*He who has my commandments
and keeps them,
he it is who loves Me;
and he who loves Me
shall be loved by My Father,
and I will love him…
…and will disclose
Myself to him.*

JOHN 14:21

DAY OF RESISTANCE

BY TYLER M. SMITH

DAY OF RESISTANCE

BY TYLER M. SMITH

WORD PRODUCTIONS

PO Box 11865, Albuquerque, NM 87192

www.wordproductions.org

Published by
WORD PRODUCTIONS LLC
Albuquerque, NM 87192

Day of Resistance
By Tyler M. Smith

ISBN: 978-0-9909245-4-8

Printed in the United States of America.

Scripture quotations taken from the New American Standard Bible®, Copyright ©1960, 1962, 1963, 1968, 1971, 1972, 1973, 1975, 1977, 1995 by The Lockman Foundation. Used by permission." (www.Lockman.org)

WORD PRODUCTIONS LLC
PO Box 11865, Albuquerque, NM 87192
www.wordproductions.org

PROLOGUE

Spring Lake Park, Omaha, Nebraska
October, 1975

"Does all this seem totally silly?" Doug let out an embarrassing laugh. His friend, Dennis, stood in front of him holding a shovel.

"Sometimes it does," Dennis answered Doug, "but in my spirit I keep sensing an urgency, and I keep asking myself if God has some purpose that we do not understand...or never will."

Doug shrugged his shoulders and nodded. "Yeah, I know. I've felt the same thing myself. We don't really have any clue what the future might hold, and what purpose this will serve." Doug also held a shovel in his hand. "So, Denny, what do you think? Is this the right spot?" Dennis nodded in the affirmative, and they started to dig.

Doug Wenger and Dennis Taylor both stood in a small clearing right in the middle of a thick grove of trees that were located a short walk from the 9th hole at Spring Lake Park, a popular golf course at the time. They figured near the 9th hole was as good a spot as any for a burial.

This was no ordinary burial, but very unusual. They were burying a fire extinguisher, of all things!

Doug and Dennis were both Bible students at the Omaha Bible Institute on 10th Street. Spring Lake Park was located about six blocks from the campus. Dennis lived across the street from the school in an old Victorian-style mansion. Altogether, six students occupied private rooms in the old wood-splintered hulk of a house.

The place was considered a fire hazard, and when Dennis's brother Robert came to visit, he decided to give Dennis a fire extinguisher for a gift. Dennis had other ideas. Dennis had grown up watching sci-fi movies, and episodes of the *Twilight Zone.* So, despite the fact that he was a well-learned, born-again Bible student, most of the people who knew him well would all agree that he was a bit "out there."

Dennis managed to break the seal on the top of the fire extinguisher, and unscrew the large cap.

This particular fire extinguisher was of the large variety, like you see in public schools, and not the small camping models that a person could purchase from the local hardware store. This one was of the serious industrial variety!

Dennis dumped all the liquid contents and thoroughly rinsed the inside of the canister. He then detached the rubber hose along with the nozzle and filled in the side opening with a welding torch to make sure it was tightly sealed. The top opening was large enough to fit books, memos, pictures and similar items into the canister. It was transformed into a makeshift time capsule.

He and his roommate, Doug, got the wild idea that the *last days* would soon come, and they wanted to share something useful to survivors when unearthed in the future world. What was more useful or important than the Holy Bible?

They filled the canister with the "New American Standard" and "King James" Bibles—three large ones with both Old and New Testaments—and several pocket size New Testaments, as well. They wrote a short memo, and dated it "October, 1975," then sealed all the contents, twisting the cap as tightly as possible. They also had a huge roll of plastic wrap that was considered non-degradable, which they wrapped in several layers, tightly around it.

Now they were at Spring Lake Park, ready to perform the burial ritual. It was a relatively shallow grave, only about four feet deep, but they managed to replace the dirt and spread leaves on top of it to make it look untouched. It was a rather sloppy job, because they had to leave the scene quickly, when they spotted a group of golfers approaching the 9th green.

As they were walking back toward the campus with shovels slung over their shoulders, Dennis smiled at Doug. "Well, silly or not, it's done! So, now we just go on with business as usual."

Within a few months Doug and Dennis both graduated and moved back to their hometowns—Dennis, to Oklahoma City, and Doug, to Hutchinson, Kansas. Within a short time, the Bible-burying project was dismissed from their thoughts.

The twenty-first century...

DAY OF RESISTANCE

PART ONE: THE BIBLE CLUB

And He was saying to them "The harvest is plentiful, but the laborers are few; therefore, beseech the Lord of the harvest to send out laborers into His harvest. Go your ways; behold, I send you out as lambs in the midst of wolves." (Luke 10:2-3)

PHIL WAS WATCHING THE CLOCK. He realized the more he watched the movement of time, the slower it seemed to move.

The lecture was boring, and he had a difficult time staying awake. This was the final class of the day, and he would be free at last! Free to meet with his friends. Finally, the professor reached the point where he would wrap things up and dole out an assignment to the students. The professor snapped his textbook closed, and faced the class. "So, by tomorrow, I'd like to see a brief essay from each of you. I want personal viewpoints, not just the standard answers. I want you to ask yourselves the question of whether or not nuclear weapons really deterred the U.S. and Soviet Union during the cold war period between the 1950's and the 1970's; and, if so, would they be a deterrent against our enemies in this present time?" Then he said those magic words. "By tomorrow! Dismissed!"

Phil bolted for the hall. Directly across that hall from Phil Jackson's classroom, his computer-nerd friend, Jennifer Houston, was leaving her final class, as well. When Phil spotted her, he quickly approached. "Where are we meeting today?" he asked her.

She leaned in close to his ear and lowered her voice. "By the picnic tables near the pavilion, and Phil, don't bring a Bible this time. I'll explain at the meeting."

Phil looked surprised. "Did you let the others know?"

She smiled, then answered, "I talked to Stu and Todd." Then, as they walked together down the hallway of the Omaha University of Nebraska, she pulled Phil aside and added, "I also invited Patty Miller. Look, I know you think she's a loose cannon, but there's a reason she needs to be there!" She smiled again. "By the way, she will be able to bring her Bible, but she is the only one." Phil looked totally confused now, but Jennifer continued to smile. "I'll explain when we get there. So, see you in about 18 minutes, okay?" She put a hand on Phil's shoulder. "It'll be all right! I'll explain when we get there... really!"

Phil left the building through the front entrance, and Jennifer by a side door near the conference room, then they finally met at Elmwood Park, near the pavilion. Stu Watson, Todd Mason, and Patty Miller came strolling over a few minutes later. They all liked meeting near the pavilion, because it was on the far end of the park where the other students didn't usually hang out.

Once they were comfortably seated at the picnic table, Stu asked, "Ok, Jenn, what's this all about? How can we get into the Word with no Bibles?"

Jennifer laughed. "Patty has a Bible." She turned to Patty. "Let me see your Bible for a moment, and I'll explain." Patty handed her Bible to Jennifer with some slight hesitation. Jennifer held it up in front of her and said, "This Bible! Let me tell you about this Bible! If I'm correct in what Patty has told me, it is an older 'King James' Bible that has been in her family since the early 70's, and has never really left her parent's house, until they gave it to her when she left home to attend school here. I refer to this as a SAFE Bible! Perhaps one of the very few safe Bibles in our possession. The others are questionable."

"Ok," Stu came back, "I don't get what you're saying…"

Jennifer then turned more serious. "I'm talking about wireless communications, Stu!" Everyone looked confused. "Every Bible sold over the last few years in a bookstore before The Church Act came into effect, had a computer chip located somewhere in the pages. A chip so small that it is close to impossible to spot! The chip transmits a signal, and gives any person with the right tech skills, a way to follow the Bible wherever it goes." Everyone was silent as Jennifer continued. "Not only that, but even a lot of older Bibles that left their owner's homes and were placed in 'Goodwills' or used bookstores, could have also been chipped, before they were sold. Those Bibles are at least questionable, and not considered safe!"

"So what do we do for now, Jen?" Phil asked.

"Well," Jen answered, "with Patty's permission, I would like each of us to bring a notebook tomorrow, and we will start copying scriptures from her Bible. I would also suggest that any Bibles you may have lying around that are not safe, give to the 'Goodwill'; leave them somewhere; destroy them, if you must; but don't use them anymore."

Patty smiled, then added, "By the way, The Church Act is pretty serious—my parents are caught up in it. The government wants all churches to register and follow certain rules on what they can and cannot teach! The I.R.S. even checks up on them. One thing that really kills me, is that churches can no longer teach that Jesus is the only way of salvation, because it leaves other religions out. So, they call it 'hate speech!' There's other stuff, too, and it's really sickening!"

Stu then spoke up. "We will need to trust the Lord to watch over us. We also need to start being more careful to depend on the Holy Spirit to lead us on who to trust or not to trust, don't you think?"

Patty sneered. "Then you better stay clear of me, if you want to stay out of trouble, Stu, because I'm going to be bold, no matter what! You can use my Bible if you like, but the rest of the time, I will carry it proudly, okay?"

Then Todd spoke. "Ok, so we bring notebooks tomorrow?"

"And we pray!" added Stu. "Oh, by the way," Stu raised his eyebrows, "I'm done with finals in a couple of weeks—I thought I'd head out to Rapid City to visit my parents. Let me know if anyone wants to tag along. I have a lead I want to follow up on with my step-dad. We're gonna go spelunking in the badlands. So, if you're up to the challenge, let me know!"

"I can't really afford it," Phil said.

"No worry," Stu replied, "I've got plenty of credit on my bankcard for expenses!"

"Shall we call it a day?" Jennifer interrupted.

"Yep," was the general answer.

"Okay, then," Phil said, "see you all tomorrow with notebooks. You, too, Patty. We need your Bible. So, please be here, okay?"

THE NEXT FEW DAYS WERE OVERWHELMING and very taxing on all of them. They had to cram every day at study periods to get their class assignments done, and give themselves as much time as possible to hand-copy scriptures after classes. Computers could not be used to type with, because even desktop information could be monitored by the N.S.A. Everything had to be handwritten. Patty would read aloud from her Bible for hours, as long as there was sunlight. They were making some progress and managed to copy the Gospel of John in four hours.

Also, every time they met it had to be outdoors. Their actions and speech could easily be observed if they were anywhere near a laptop computer or cell phone. They had to make sure that the bare-bones of pen and paper, along with Patty's Bible, were all they had on their persons when they met by the pavilion.

Because of The Church Act, Christians had to comply with government regulations by first being registered, then by following a set of rules regarding what was taught from the pulpit.

Homosexuality as a sin was unlawful to teach publicly. Jesus as the only Savior could no longer be taught. Anything that violated the government's idea of human rights, much of which was taught in Scripture, was unlawful to proclaim! Those who did follow the Bible and set themselves apart from church registration were considered cults.

Registered churches were also limited to using only textbooks regulated by the Government. A religious board of scholars was called together to compile a new bible, called "The Common Bible," which incorporated teachings from all of the mainstream world religions into one text that blended the teachings into one universal viewpoint. Original translations of the Bible, such as King James, New American Standard, or N.I.V., could no longer be used in churches.

Under all this hubbub, our college campus Christian friends were in violation of just about every religious law in America, enough to even face a death sentence. In this future world, America no longer tolerated "crimes against humanity."

When laws were violated, the violators were executed, in most cases. The 5th Amendment no longer existed, nor did rights to a phone call or an attorney.

Members of the police force, F.B.I., and any other institution funded by the Government made their own determination regarding the guilt or innocence of those accused of crimes.

Finally, one day only two weeks away from summer break, Stu again approached Phil and the others about a road trip to Rapid City.

"So, what's this business about caves?" Phil asked him.

"Well," Stu explained, "in the badlands there are a lot of caves. My stepfather and I are trying to find just the right one to be a future place of refuge. One we could stock up with food, supplies, safe Bibles, and other needs, and make it a livable place for a handful of believers!" He paused a moment, then continued. "Things are bound to get worse, and we will all need a place to go when it does! What is nice, is that it is not unusual for me to take trips to South Dakota, because everyone knows I'm going there to visit my folks."

"Well," Phil answered, "you don't have to wait for things to get worse, 'cause they already GOT worse!" Phil then looked at Patty Miller. "And you! Hey, what's this I hear about an incident in your philosophy class? I heard that you stood up and bellowed at the professor for excluding the belief in Jesus Christ, and told him that those who didn't repent would go to hell! You also told the class that rejection of Christ was the main reason for the decay of society. Is that true?"

Patty stood her ground. "You bet it's true! Hey, look, we are sheep in the midst of wolves! Jesus was considered a lamb led to the slaughter, and He chose the cross! Jesus taught us to follow the will of our Father God, to proclaim the Gospel, even though we may suffer and die for it! Is that not true, Phil?"

"Yes," Phil agreed. "However, the Bible also teaches not to cast your pearls before swine, and there is a reason for that, as well! Also, we are to be crafty as foxes, yet gentle as doves, and remember, Patty, that even Jesus didn't blast it everywhere! He used some discretion. If you get arrested, Patty, it will also shine a suspicious light on your friends here—your Bible and our handwritten copies of the Word will be confiscated as well. We will have gained nothing!"

Patty only shook her head slightly and said, "Break's over now. We'd better get back to work." The subject was dropped for the time being, but it would certainly be brought up again soon. Jennifer did not get involved in any of these verbal exchanges. She was still focused on one thing—getting the Bible copied.

SUMMER BREAK WAS FINALLY right at the door, and it was good timing. The group of park pavilion Christians had managed to obtain all of their own personal handwritten copies of the New Testament. They decided to have one final get-together before the two-and-a-half month vacation from campus life. They met in their usual spot at the picnic table.

Stu started the conversation. "I've got a conviction on my heart, and it's been nagging me for some time." Everyone was attentive to what he was about to say. "Ok, it's like this," he began with a solemn look. "We've got the New Testament now, and that's a good thing, but we need to remind ourselves of the purpose it serves. We need to be in prayer and sensitive to the Spirit's leading on evangelism. The Lord's will is for us to share the Gospel with others, even though the world is against it. We can have faith that God will protect us and open doors for the Gospel to be proclaimed."

"That's what I mean!" Patty interrupted.

"Ok," Stu went on, "I get that, Patty, and I know there has been some contentions between you and Phil here, but I think the Lord has given some guidance on these things."

"I certainly hope so!" Jennifer smiled. "I'm a little tired of hearing these two go at it all the time."

"Well," Stu spoke again, "really they are both right! In the book of Acts, the apostles prayed for more boldness, even though they had already been jailed for boldness. In the 7th Chapter, we have the proclamation of Stephen, which ended in his death! Ah, but before he died, he had seen Jesus standing at the right hand of the Father to receive him into heaven, and it is written that his face appeared as the face of an angel! In the Gospel of Matthew, Jesus told His disciples that they would be blessed when persecuted, and that their rewards would be great in heaven. We have all been taught to seek those rewards that are above, and not on the earth! So, all of these things are indications that Patty has a valid conviction. Now hear me out!" Stu paused to be sure that everyone was listening. "Phil also has a valid conviction! You see, there are two ways to evangelize. One is by the flesh, which can be done in an attitude of defiance, or in the Spirit, which is done in an attitude of love. The motivation of the flesh can be reckless and lack a genuine care for others. The Holy Spirit produces the fruit of the Spirit—love, joy, peace, patience, kindness, goodness—which we've all read together in the book of Galatians. The Spirit of God will also lead us in the direction of His perfect will. A good example is in the fifth Chapter of John. You might recall the paralytic who sat by the pool of Bethesda. Well, as you know, people gathered by that pool by the hundreds, yet that particular man was the one Jesus went to and healed! Also, Jesus warned his disciples of a time they would be dragged before governors and kings, and that it would be God in the person of the Holy Spirit that would do the talking through them, so they need not bother to drum up any words in their own defense! We need both, folks! We need to understand

Phil's point about being careful to do all things in the Spirit with sound discretion. We also need Patty's kind of zeal, and not shrink back from our duty to preach the Gospel. In other words, don't let the crap in this world stop you! I love you both, and I hope this is settled and that you two will pray together and become one mind and heart, because the same Holy Spirit lives in all of us. That's it! I got it all said; thanks for listening." Stu folded his arms across his chest and sat back to relax.

Patty and Phil stood up and embraced. There were tears in Patty's eyes. They embraced for a long time, while the others prayed over them.

"With all that said and done," Phil said, smiling at Stu, "I decided, after praying about it, to go with you to South Dakota. I called my folks and told them I would try to make it home to Illinois when I got back. They're cool with it."

Stu smiled back and nodded. "Welcome aboard! I don't understand everything my step-dad has in mind, but my heart is open. Hey, we're flyin' Dude! I'll pick up the tickets this afternoon. Dad will pick us up at the airport in Rapid City!"

Patty decided to stay with her sister, Susan, in Lincoln. She couldn't see being around her parents when they had gotten so caught up in the government-run church. She was afraid she might say something she would regret.

Todd and Jennifer would be going home to their families. Todd, to Kansas City, and Jennifer's family lived right in Omaha.

"How about we close with something from the Word?" Todd said. Stu smiled and so did Patty.

"What do you have for us, Todd?" Patty asked while brushing back her hair.

Todd picked up his notebook and fumbled a bit, because the pages were sticking together. Everyone laughed. "Oh, here it is," Todd was red with embarrassment. "Ah, okay," Todd cleared his throat. "Yes, here it is from John 15..."

> *"This is my commandment, that ye love one another as I have loved you. Greater love hath no man than this, that a man lay down his life for his friends, if ye do whatsoever I command you. Henceforth, I call you not servants; for the servant knoweth not what his Lord doeth: but I have called you friends; for all things that I have heard from my Father, I have made known unto you. You have not chosen me, but I have chosen you, and ordained you, that ye should go and bring forth fruit, and that your fruit should remain: that whatsoever ye shall ask of the Father in my name, He may give it to you. These things I command you, that ye love one another."*

Todd then gently closed his notebook Bible and proceeded to return it to his backpack. Everyone gathered around Todd and they all embraced. The Lord had spoken to them through His Word.

"So," Jennifer sighed, "see you all next semester, I guess." They all parted ways, and headed back to campus to pack and register for the next semester's classes.

4
CHAPTER

STU AND PHILLIP SAT OFF TO THE SIDE AT GATE 22. They found a couple of seats where they figured it would be safe enough to talk. They had about an hour to kill before their flight to Rapid City was due to board.

Stu leaned toward Phil and quietly said, "I think it's a good idea for you to know who my stepfather is, so that you are prepared. You would recognize the name, I'm sure. He's Reverend Timothy Harris."

"You're kidding me!" Phillip responded with a look of shock on his face, "the Timothy Harris that got involved in that controversy a few years back?"

Stu nodded. "That's him."

Phil looked puzzled. "I don't really remember it that well, but I do know it had to do with a statement he made about Muslims, right?"

Stu nodded in the affirmative.

"So, what happened, Stu?" "Well," Stu began, "he said in an interview that there was really no difference between the so-called moderate Muslims and the radicals. A moderate Muslim happened to also be a guest on the same show, and went ballistic! In the end, my step-dad was ridiculed by the news media, and pretty much lost everything."

"So, do you agree?" Phil then asked.

Stu thought for a moment before he answered. "From the standpoint of the Bible, yes, I do! It's written in John's first Epistle that any spirit that does not confess Jesus Christ is come in the flesh is not of God. It goes so far as to say that any spirit that doesn't confess Jesus is the spirit of Antichrist! Also, Paul taught that Satan disguises himself as an angel of light, and his demons as ministers of righteousness! So, yes, I agree with my dad on that."

Stu took a breath and continued. "My step-dad believes the only difference is that radicals act out their hatred physically, where moderates keep it in their hearts. No Muslim acknowledges Jesus as the Son of God, or that He died for sin and was resurrected. Jesus said he who is not for Him is against Him. He who does not gather, scatters! This brings only one conclusion—that all Muslims are against Christ. They may say they love Him as a prophet, but still refuse to see Him for who He really is."

Phil's eyes widened. "I'm really looking forward to meeting your step-dad—it's amazing he wasn't jailed for his views."

Stu chuckled. "Today, he would go to the wall, I'm sure—back in the day this happened, America still had free speech. Nowadays, he keeps a low profile, but you can almost bet that The Church Act fanatics are watching him."

Right at that time, the intercom blared. "Flight 370 for Rapid City is now boarding at gate 22." This was repeated 3 times.

The flight went smoothly without a hitch, and after a slightly bumpy landing, Reverend Timothy Harris was waiting for them at the gate.

The Harris home was amazing! It was located about 12 miles out of town, in a small, private community. A ranch-style cabin made of good old-fashioned logs. The décor inside was unique, because it was of old style design and nothing new or modern at all. He did have a CD player, however. It was housed inside of an old radio console from the early 1950s. He had a unique collection of music from the 20s to the 50s, plus a collection of vintage radio shows from the 40s. His television was an old Zenith, with a DVD player hidden inside the cabinet. His DVD collection consisted of old TV series like *I Love Lucy* and *Dragnet*. Also, a collection of Billy Graham crusades.

On the drive from the airport, Stu filled him in about the Bible chipping situation. Tim Harris already knew a lot about the N.S.A.'s technology of spying through computers and cell phones, but wasn't aware of Bible chipping. He was safe anyway, because he only owned two Bibles, both of which he had owned for many years.

"Why buy a new one, when the old one works just fine?" He said. The newest Bible was purchased in 1978. Timothy had no computer, not even a laptop, and no telephone. He made and received all calls on the phone at Frank's hardware store down the road, and in phone conversations, he was always careful to keep it discreet.

When Stu and Phil arrived, Stu's mother, Nancy, already had a huge spread for dinner—ham, scalloped potatoes, cornbread, and Dutch apple pie. Nancy Harris was still recovering from a stroke she had had a few months back, so her ability to communicate was limited. The dinner must have taken all day to prepare.

After dinner, Tim and his guests retired into the living room and discussed all the things they needed to catch up on. Phil told him all about the fellowship in Omaha, and how they had all copied the New Testament by hand. Stu commented on what a blessing it was to be in the cabin where there were two safe Bibles.

Reverend Harris didn't launch into much talk about his past ministry, but mostly spoke of a cave he found in the Badlands. "I think it's the perfect one we're looking for, Stuart. It has three entrances and it's elevated in the cliffs—it's on Indian land, but I know the people, and they're willing to share."

Before turning in for a good night's sleep, Tim dug out a CD containing the original *War of the Worlds* broadcast. Phil and Stu both laughed while listening and wondered how anyone could take those fake news reports seriously. Tim later explained that in the 1940s, the news reports really DID sound that strange. They spoke like used car salesmen or carnival barkers.

Phil was delighted with Reverend Harris—Tim Harris was so warm, knowledgeable and entertaining. They retired that night about 11:30. Bright and early in the morning, they would decide about a possible trip to the Badlands.

IT WAS ABOUT 10 P.M. THE NEXT NIGHT that the phone started ringing at Jennifer's parents' home. "Jen," her mother called from the kitchen, "some gal is calling you from Lincoln."

Jennifer clicked off the television. "Ok, comin,' Mom!" She entered the kitchen and reached for the phone in her mother's hand. "Probably Patty, my friend from school," she said.

Jennifer put the receiver to her ear. "That you, Patty?"

A panicky voice answered her on the other end. "This is Sue Miller, Patty's sister, we've got trouble! You're Jennifer, right?"

Jen remained calm. "Yeah, that's me—what's going on? Are you crying?"

Sue paused to gain her composure. "Patty just got arrested!" She started to cry again. "She couldn't get away from her e-mails, and got angry. She ended up posting anti-government stuff on the Net. She also blasted out some radical religious statements to the wrong people. She was traced and the cops picked her up. She kept yelling at me to call you when she was dragged out the door!"

"Oh, that's just great!" Jennifer flatly spoke in a sarcastic tone. "What else could you find out?"

Sue's voice trembled in her ear. "Well I followed her down to the police station in my car, but they wouldn't let me see her. After about two hours, a cop came up to tell me she was going to be sent to Scottsbluff."

Jennifer was horrified by that name—"Scottsbluff." It was the location in the Nebraska Panhandle where death sentences were carried out. "Look, Sue, I'll make some calls. Try to calm down and wait for me to call you back, okay?"

"Thank you, Jen," Sue was still crying when she hung up.

Jennifer disconnected the call and quickly dialed a number that Stu gave her to reach him in case of emergency. It seemed like forever for the party she was calling to finally pick up!

"Yep," was the answer on the other end.

"Is this Frank from the hardware store?" Jennifer's voice was shaky.

The man on the other end answered, "That's me. Hey, I'm fixin' to close up, so make it fast."

"I'm calling for Stuart Watson," Jen responded. "Tim Harris's stepson. It's an emergency! This is the number he gave me."

Frank asked the usual question. "And who is calling?"

"I'm Jennifer, from Omaha! We go to the same school. Please, sir, this is an emergency."

"Ok, calm down, little miss, Tim's cabin is only five minutes away—I'll run over and get him, so he can call you right back. There's no phone at Tim's house—he'll have to use mine. So, just stay put and I'll do what I can. Does he know your number?"

"Yes, yes, please hurry!"

"I'm on my way now," Frank said, then he quickly hung up the phone and ran outside to his truck.

Jennifer was on the verge of a panic attack when ten minutes had gone by with no call back. Finally when it reached 15 minutes, the phone rang. Jennifer nearly jumped out of her skin!

"Hello, is this Stu?"

"Yes, Jen, what's going on?" His voice comforted her, yet she still broke down in tears.

"It's Patty...and it's bad! She got arrested and accused of some hate crime and some plot against the government. They're sending her to the wall, Stu!"

"Ok, okay, listen now." Stu answered. "Calm down and listen carefully, you can't do anything to help her right now. I know that sounds uncaring, but if you try to get involved, you might end up going down with her. You gotta stay clear for now. This is what I need you to do, Jen—call Todd in Kansas City. I'll call him, too."

Stu thought for a moment, then continued. "We've got to figure out a way to get you both to Rapid City without being detected!"

"What, Stu? I don't get it!" She was calmer now.

"When someone like Patty gets busted, they will go after their friends also. How did you find out about this?"

Jen told him, "Patty's sister, Susan, called."

"Ok, then," Stu went on. "Get hold of her, too—we need to get all of you out of there—you'll need to ditch your IDs. Transportation will be the hard part. My dad will probably come up with something."

Jennifer began to cry again. "But what about school? Man!"

Stu didn't know how to answer. "We'll talk about it later, Jen—for now, just call Todd, all right?"

Down at police headquarters, Patty Miller waited in a holding cell. The local judge for that district was touring the facility at that time in order to review criminal cases. When it was Patty's turn to enter the interrogation room, she sat across the table from the arresting officer and the judge.

When questioned by the judge about her hate speech crime, plus her public denouncements against the government, Patty was hostile and uncooperative. She ended up screaming at the judge that he would go to hell for rejecting Christ. When the judge rose to leave, he was gravely offended. He turned toward the arresting officer, shook his head as if he was trying to show pity, and said, "Scottsbluff." He had a slight catch in his throat. "I'm sorry, Miss Miller." Then he repeated to the officer, "Scottsbluff." He then quietly left the room.

Now at this point, it was probably going to take a couple of days for the police to find out who Patty's friends were from school, so the chances were good that the conversations from Jennifer's phone were not monitored. Jennifer prayed about it, none the less. She had peace that everything would be all right for now.

Jennifer tried for two hours to get through to Todd in Kansas City. His phone was constantly dropping her calls to voice mail. She finally got through at 1:00 a.m., and found out he'd been on the line with Stu and Tim Harris the whole time.

"Here's the plan," Todd told Jen. "I'm getting ready to leave for Lincoln right now. I want you and Susan to meet me in Lincoln at the Capitol building at noon tomorrow, got that?"

"Ok," Jen answered. "We can get there."

"Great," Todd continued. "Inside the Capitol Lobby is a coffee shop—meet me there. I'll tell you the rest when we get there. After you call Susan, stay off the phone! I'll see you in Lincoln." Then he hung up.

CHAPTER

THE THREE OF THEM MADE IT SAFELY to the Capitol building right on time. There were quite a few visitors that day, which was good, because then they didn't stand out.

They spotted Todd in front of the coffee shop, but none of them went in. Instead, Todd led them out of the crowd and motioned for them to step outside and stand in front of the main entrance. Todd said, "Okay, now we keep our eyes on the street. There should be a gold Jeep Cherokee circling the block—when we spot it, we get in." No one questioned the plan.

Sure enough, they spotted the gold Jeep turning the corner and slowing down next to the curb; in the next block, it came to a stop. Todd, Jen, and Sue quickly walked over to it, opened the back door, and slid in. The driver was a woman, perhaps in her late 40s with slightly greying hair. She smiled when they entered the Jeep. "I'm Angela, and you are?"

Todd answered, "Jennifer, Susan, and Todd."

"Good!" She nodded. "I'm Tim Harris' younger sister. He called me last night and told me the whole story. I visit him quite a bit in Rapid City, so I can provide safe travel. I'm also legal, and still carry a bankcard. Now, here's what we need to do." She passed a plastic trash bag to the back seat. "All bankcards, IDs, driver's licenses, cell phones or any other items that are electronic go into the bag...which will go into a trash receptacle on the corner up there. If authorities decide to do any tracking, the trail will end here in Lincoln, Nebraska! I will be keeping my own things, because I need to stay legal, so we can travel without suspicion."

They all began to discard the few items they had into the trash bag. "Susan? What's your story? Since you are Patty Miller's sister." Angela wanted to know.

Susan hesitantly answered, "Well, ah, I'm supposed to report to the police station today at two o'clock for more questioning. Ah, they wanna know more of Patty's background."

Angela smiled. "Well, I guess that is one appointment you'll miss!"

Jennifer began to look scared. Todd took her hand gently and Jennifer accepted it. Then she began to cry and spoke through her tears. "Does this mean we cease to exist? I was hoping to finish school!"

Angela gave her a grim look. "That is all over, Jenny, if you try to resume your life as before, the authorities will find out you were connected with Patty! You'll be questioned, and arrested. They will identify you as a cultist!"

Angela continued, this time speaking to all of them. "Here's the deal, people. Have you ever heard of the Witness Protection Program? Well, this is similar to that. Your past life is done! Your past family is done! You will contact NO ONE! You'll make no phone calls or use a computer. If there are any purchases to make, Tim or I will make them for the time being." Then her voice softened and she spoke tenderly with love: "Please understand and know that we all belong to the Lord Jesus. We walk by faith from now on. His rewards are not of this world. We must pray for knowledge of His will for us, and follow by faith. 'The old things have passed away, behold! All things have become new!' By the way, speaking of the Lord, do any of you have Bibles in your backpacks? Any that you have purchased within the last ten years?"

"Not Todd or I," Jennifer answered. "We found out about the chipping of books, so we only have hand written versions of the Word."

"Okay," Angela went on. "You're safe then. What about you, Susan?"

Sue shrugged. "The cops took my sister's family Bible, so I've got nothing."

"Alrighty, then." Angela pointed to the trash bag. "Todd? Do you want to do the honors?"

Todd stepped out of the vehicle and quickly deposited the bag in the street corner trash receptacle, and returned to the Jeep.

"All right, we're on our way, then!" Angela comforted everyone with a loving smile as she pulled away from the curb and drove toward the entrance ramp to jump on the interstate.

WHEN THEY FIRST ARRIVED at the Harris residence, they needed to devise a plan concerning Stuart and Phillip's IDs, bankcards and traceable location. They also would be connected to Patty Miller in due time.

Angela came up with a workable plan. She had Stu and Phil put their bankcards and IDs in an envelope. She would carry the cards with her on the return trip to Nebraska. If a signal was traced, it would appear that she was giving them a ride back to Omaha. She would stop in Omaha and discard the IDs, then return to Lincoln. When it became obvious that they had disappeared, the authorities would assume they discarded the IDs when they returned, and went into hiding somewhere in Nebraska or Iowa. The trail would end in Omaha, and lead nowhere.

If Angela was questioned after returning to Lincoln, she would just play dumb! It would be the truth if she said she didn't know Patty Miller. Her nephew and his friend simply needed a ride back to Omaha to the college campus apartment they shared.

Once Angela left Rapid City, Tim decided it was time for a serious meeting. Tim's plan to house renegade Christians was already in the works—just a lot sooner than he had expected!
After a few days had passed, Agent Lawrence Bloomfield, who

worked for the FBI office in Omaha, connected the dots that led him to believe that Stuart Watson and Phillip Jackson had some type of association with Patty Miller. He found out about the airline tickets to Rapid City, and after some phone calls finally contacted Gabriel Lewis, known as "Gabe," who was head of the Sheriff's Department in Rapid City, South Dakota. Bloomfield didn't realize at the time that Gabe was a close friend of Tim Harris, and was also a born-again Christian. After discussing the case on the phone, Gabe assured Bloomfield that he would question Reverend Harris on the matter.

With the discovery that Patty's friends had discarded their IDs, Bloomfield had assumed they'd gone into hiding. Before Bloomfield ever called, Gabe and Tim had already discussed it. They got a story together that they could agree on. During Stu and Phil's stay with Tim, they'd never once mentioned Patty Miller, which was true! (It was true in the sense that they'd returned home in Angela's Jeep—at least their IDs did. Angela was not told by them about Patty Miller which was true again. She was not filled in on the purpose for the trip to Rapid City at the time.) She knew about Patty Miller, but she'd gotten that information from Tim, not her passengers. Until she provided them with a ride, she had never met Todd, Jennifer, or Susan. Gabe would assure Bloomfield that the Reverend Harris was still not active in political or religious organizations since the 1980s. True, again!

After Bloomfield called a second time to find out what Gabe had learned from Tim Harris, he was finally convinced to close that part of the investigation. The whole issue was a needle in a haystack, as far as finding the whereabouts of Patty Miller's friends.

THE TRIP TO THE BADLANDS that Reverend Harris had planned for the morning after Stu and Phil's arrival was postponed because they needed one more day to get situated. After news of Patty's arrest, it was delayed again, until the others arrived safely.

When they did arrive, it was late in the evening, so they spent that night having fellowship and sharing Scripture from God's Word.

Jennifer, Susan, and Todd were all distressed by what had happened to Patty. Jennifer was the one having the most struggle with the situation, and harbored a lot of anger toward Patty! "Why did she do this? Didn't she realize she would be dragging us down with her? Because of her, I won't finish school, and I'm separated from my family!" Jennifer complained.

Todd was not bothered so much, even after Jennifer blurted those words. Secretly, he really didn't care whether he finished school or not, if it meant living in a world where Christians were in constant danger! Stu was, more or less, still in a state of shock!

Reverend Harris had a safe New American Standard Bible, so they all had access to the Old Testament, which was a blessing. The Lord led them all to a passage in Isaiah 54, which was both a warning and a comfort. The Lord was speaking to the Jews, who, during those days, were going through a lot of testing and hardship. God had to constantly remind them of His faithfulness. Isaiah 54:7-8 read, as follows:

> *"For a brief moment, I forsook you, but with great compassion I will gather you. In an outburst of anger, I hid My face from you for a moment. But with everlasting loving kindness, I will have compassion on you, says the Lord, your Redeemer."*

They all realized that this applied to all of them, as well as the Jews. Jennifer also found forgiveness in her heart, realizing it also applied to Patty Miller. They all joined together in prayer for Patty, that God would deliver her by His compassionate love.

That same night, Reverend Harris made a quick run to the general hardware store to use Frank's phone. Tim placed a call to Johnny Rainwater, who lived on the Cedar Ridge Indian Reservation. Although Johnny Rainwater was a pure Oglala Lakota Indian, he was quite a character. Johnny was from the old school, and knew a lot about the history of the region. He did NOT like to be called a "Native American," because to him, a Native American was a liberal socialist who wanted to be called Native American for political correctness. Johnny would rather be referred to as an American Indian (or even an Injun or a Redskin) before he would accept a name assigned by America's newfangled language.

The Cedar Ridge Reservation was thought by many to be a slum, but the one advantage to living on Indian land was that they had little or no interference from the U.S. Government!

Reverend Tim made arrangements with Johnny that night, to stop by his cabin in the morning, and accompany them all to the caves. Johnny and Reverend Harris had been good friends for years, and Johnny Rainwater was willing to help in any way he could.

9
CHAPTER

Johnny Rainwater showed up bright and early the next morning, and they all had breakfast together at Tim's cabin. After breakfast, they all loaded up Tim's old panel truck. Tim knew exactly where the location was that he was interested in. Jennifer, Phil, and Todd had to ride in the back, and the journey was not exactly pleasant! The trail was rocky and pitted. It took about a half hour to reach the area. They had crossed into Indian land when the truck finally came to a stop. Everyone was relieved to get out and stretch.

"Right up there!" Reverend Harris pointed to a location fairly high up into the rock cliffs. About midway up the face of the cliff, they could plainly see three cave entrances.

"Yes," Johnny Rainwater stated. "I know this place well. For generations we called them "the caves of fear." Our ancestors would fast for many days and then enter those caves to speak to the spirits. Mostly they were simply hallucinating from several days of no food and water. They saw visions and the spirits would reveal to them the secrets of their deepest fears. Hence the name."

Todd quietly commented to Phil, "I'll bet they're full of bats!"

Although they stood quite a distance from Johnny, they were surprised to see him turn toward them, and shout, "No! No bats!"

Todd was amazed and walked over to Johnny. "You could hear me from way over there?"

Rainwater smiled and answered "In our tribe, we all grew up from childhood learning to listen and fine tune our hearing skills. Our fathers were hunters, and most could put an arrow straight through the heart of a deer, even when the deer was hidden from view in the shadows, just by hearing alone."

"So, you are a hunter?" Phil asked.

"No," Rainwater answered. "I keep my ears in shape mostly so I can listen to classic rock music on KFOR FM. I'm into Creedence Clearwater Revival more than deer."

Everyone laughed. "So?" Reverend Harris spoke. "What do you know about the caves, John?"

"They are all interconnected," Rainwater explained, "there are several passageways that connect one cave to another. All three of them only go back about a hundred yards, then they all end in one large opening on the other side of the cliff. Some of the early dwellers drilled through the top ceiling in various places, so that fresh air would filter in. I'm still amazed they could punch all the way through all that rock to reach the top of the cliff."

Jennifer looked fascinated and asked Johnny. "So are there really bats in there, or not?"

Johnny smiled. "No, just like I said, 'no bats.' Probably because these caves are too dry and most bats like moisture. Although the ancients believed the bats were chased out by spirits!"

Jennifer responded in a shaky voice. "Spirits? That sounds so creepy! What kind of spirits?"

Rainwater continued, "The ancients believed they were spirits of ancestors, and also spirits of fear and evil. Definitely not the Holy Spirit! I, myself, believe it was probably legend more than reality, but," he shrugged, "I've been brainwashed by white culture, in their opinion. Do you want to go in and check it out?"

Reverend Harris scratched his head. "Before we do that, Johnny, I've got the million dollar question. How will the spiritual leaders in your tribe take to the idea of us using these caves?"

Rainwater laughed. "We haven't talked to the spirits for years in these caves; we have no important use for them now. I will warn them that we have palefaces in our midst." He laughed again. "You'll be safe on Indian land, Tim, and there won't be any threat from the government's interference. Even the FBI is not comfortable on our land. We have the right to maintain our own laws and culture, as long as we don't interfere with those outside our boundaries." Rainwater slapped Tim on the back and smiled. "You are welcome, my friends. As Jesus said, 'Let not your heart be troubled.'"

"So how about that tour?" Phil then asked.

"There is a rock trail that will lead you up to the caves, however, I think we should delay," Rainwater answered. "Tomorrow, I'll send up a couple of climbers, just to make sure everything is solid up there. Sound good?"

They all nodded yes. Finally they headed back to Tim's cabin, as Rainwater went on his way as well.

"So," Tim asked his friends. "What do you think?"

"Only one thing bothers me, Dad," Stu answered, "I feel a little funny about hiding in caves! Like, instead of preaching the Gospel and facing the music, we're hiding in caves?"

"That's a valid concern, son," Tim smiled. "So we need to do some serious praying. I think God will give us plenty of work ministering to those on the reservation, but we'll see."

CHAPTER

10

THAT NIGHT AFTER A HEALTHY DINNER, everyone gathered in the living room for a community meeting. Tim Harris decided it was time to address some issues he felt that his guests needed to have cleared up in their minds.

"My stepson, here, brought a very valid concern to my attention today after we visited the caves," he began. "He was concerned about Christians like us, hiding our lights under a bushel and living in caves. I just thought I'd put your minds at ease on that. Hopefully, none of us will be living in caves any time soon. I only intend to get them prepared for future use. I have reason to believe that chaos is coming to this country soon. I mean things such as anarchy, plagues, war, and judgements! I'm no expert on prophecy or the books of Revelation, but common sense along with spiritual sense tells me things are quickly leading that way."

Tim paused a moment to be sure everyone was listening closely, then he continued. "Because of the government's oversight in not securing the border between the U.S. and Mexico, many others besides just Mexican refugees have crossed over—like the cartels! Also, thousands of radical Muslim enemies from the Middle East live among us, as well! No doubt they will eventually make a move to overthrow America, and when that day comes, there will be bloodshed like never before. Mostly the blood of

Jews and Christians! So, I believe that it is the calling of God for my life, to prepare the caves for a place of refuge for when that time comes. Right now, I choose not to question it. I must gather literature, food, medicine, and other items for survival. For now, Johnny Rainwater says he is in need of volunteers to help at the reservation. He needs a teacher at the school house for the young-uns; someone also to lead Bible Studies at the Chapel. I, myself, would appreciate anyone who can take time to look after my wife, Nancy. Not long ago, she suffered a serious stroke. She still can hardly speak, but on good days, she still likes to stay active. She needs someone to help guide her along, and also someone to read to her at night. She deeply loves the Lord, and the Lord's people, but she is very limited in what she can do."

Susan smiled when Tim said that. "Sounds like the right thing for me—I can do that, for sure!" She volunteered. Jennifer then chimed in, also. "I can teach—I love children, and I have a way with them. Count me in at the School!"

Tim smiled broadly, then went on. "So that leaves Stu, Phil, and Todd—you three yokels! I hope you will help at the caves, and maybe do the Bible classes in your spare time. Sound good?"

All three mumbled in agreement, but didn't look too thrilled about the CAVE part of the deal!

Tim continued. "Now, there is also the matter of our good buddy with the FBI, in Omaha. He's looking for all of you yokels, yes, but all he knows right now is that you ditched your IDs and could be anywhere. Good ol' Lawrence Bloomfield! He doesn't think you're here now, because the only person he communicates with is our friendly 'head of the Sheriff's Department' Gabe Lewis! Gabe's got our backs covered, and Bloomfield has no reason to doubt him. However, if Bloomfield for any reason sends any of his agents here to snoop around, we can only hope that Rainwater and Gabe will both know about it. God is watching over us ultimately...you all know that! Johnny told me if we cross over into Indian land, his community would protect us—and chances are they would never find us. Rainwater will know what to do, trust me."

The meeting went on until midnight, and as a result, everyone managed to unwind enough to get a decent night's sleep. The next morning would be the beginning of a new life. Before turning in that night, they read John 15 together, and earnestly prayed for the Lord's direction.

"Let's stop at Frank's place first; it might save us some time by not having to go all the way to Rapid City." Tim Harris and his stepson, Stu, were beginning to gather supplies, even though it would be awhile before the caves were ready for storage. John Rainwater stopped by Tim's cabin that morning to let everyone know that all was safe up in the cliffs where the caves were located.

Rainwater also encouraged Jennifer to ride back with him to Cedar Ridge, and check things out. Johnny had already arranged some space for a small school room, directly in back of his office. In the meantime, Tim, Stu, Phil, and Todd all piled into Tim's old panel truck, and headed down the bumpy trail toward Frank's Hardware and Supply Store. When they arrived, Phil and Todd jumped down from the back of the truck, as Tim and Stu emerged from the front.

As they entered Frank's place, they noticed it was in a bit of disarray, but Frank smiled and assured them he knew where every item was located. "Hey, Reverend, good to see you!" Frank extended his hand.

"Well, I finally came to give you business, Frank." Tim answered with a chuckle.

Frank's face displayed an exaggerated look of shock. "You mean, you really came to BUY something?"

"Well," Tim dug a folded piece of paper out of his back pocket. "It depends! I wrote a list, as you can see." He handed the list over to Frank. It read as follows:

1. Five Kerosene Lanterns
2. Five Battery powered lanterns, and long-lasting lithium batteries
3. 12 gauge shotgun, 22 Cal. Rifle, lever action 30.06 and shells for all three
4. Binoculars: highest power in stock
5. Space blankets
6. Flares
7. Safe Bibles

Frank smiled. "I can do all of this except the Bibles, of course."

"Just wishful thinking," Tim replied.

"It's kind of a short list, Reverend." Frank scratched his chin.

Tim smiled at him. "Just little by little, as we can afford it."

Frank began locating items, and spoke to them from the other side of the shelves. "You'll need a lot of things, after what I heard on the news reports this morning—lots of crazy stuff, Reverend!"

Tim looked concerned. "What crazy stuff, Frank?"

Frank spoke up. "They're starting to chip people, Tim! Already doin' it in Washington, New York, and Boston. Yep, they're getting rid of the bankcards, and putting computer chips in people's bodies. Can you imagine that, Tim?"

Tim blinked his eyes and shook his head, as if in disbelief. His mouth went dry, and he didn't know what to say in response.

Finally, his stepson, Stu, walked over to him, and gently squeezed his shoulder, saying, "Well, I guess it's coming, Dad."

Frank spoke again. "Then to top it off, it's been confirmed that those in the Mideast are making nuclear threats against the U.S.! The rest of the news was pretty much the same ol' stuff. The National Guard has been deployed in Wyoming, because of that crazy quarantine. They're not sayin' nothing about the actual disease, though! It's controversy over the firing squads in Scottsbluff, the conditions of the homeless camps—same ol' stuff, Tim."

The mention of firing squads in Scottsbluff, Nebraska, brought looks of sadness to their faces. Everyone was still wondering what was going to happen to Patty Miller.

Frank suddenly brightened. "Hey, I just got a divine revelation about those Bibles on your list, Tim!"

He went on to explain. "You might want to go on into Rapid City. They got a store on 28th Street, called Used Vintage Office Supply and Collectibles. There are people who collect old office stuff, believe it or not! This place even has an old wire recorder from the 1940s. They also got a ton of manual typewriters, the good ol' standard kind, and carbon paper. If you picked up four decent typewriters, and used 'em with carbon paper, you could type two copies of the Bible on each one. With four people typin,' you'd get eight copies of the Word!"

Tim clapped his hands together. "Brilliant, Frank!" Tim hadn't really planned a trip into Rapid City that day, but after hearing about the microchipping of humans, he was now much more compelled. "Yeah! I'm goin' into town, Frank!"

Tim looked at the other three. "What do you guys think?"

Stu, Phil, and Todd all looked excited. "You bet, we oughta' do it, Dad! No doubt in my mind!" Stu stated. Then they started quickly loading the goods they had purchased from Frank.

Back on the reservation, Jennifer sat on a wooden chair in John Rainwater's office to discuss the school situation. Johnny first explained to her that he was basically the coordinator in charge of the reservation, and what he said was law, in Cedar Ridge.

When John's truck had passed over on to Indian land that morning, Jennifer had been shocked by what she had seen of Cedar Ridge. It had many faces. In one section, a very modern style community center was quite impressive. As they got deeper into the village, it turned to gutted old trailers with littered yards of weeds and trash, in which children played, and ran around in ragged underwear.

The older folks sat around on ragged lawn chairs not doing much of anything, some seeming depressed. Then appeared a huge field of tee-pees, an actual tee-pee community where Native Americans dressed in traditional clothing with feathered headdresses like the days of the old west. Johnny explained to her that many of their residents still practiced the old traditions of their forefathers. Many of them made ornaments and wood carvings to sell to tourists, while entertaining them with traditional dances and rituals.

John's office was scattered with papers, pens, and handwritten documents. A small air conditioner was in the front window, and a couple of space heaters were stored in the back corner, near his cot. The walls were covered with Native American artwork and animal skins. Also, a stuffed buffalo head hung over the doorway.

"Sorry about the mess," Johnny exclaimed. "We used to have a computer and some nice office equipment in this room. We got rid of it all in 2012, when all of the wireless tech started being used to monitor people! We are a private people, we have our own laws, and our own way of life, Jen. We try to get along as best we can, as a family."

John then led her through a doorway in the back of the building. "I know it's not much right now, but here it is!" Jennifer saw a fairly large room with a few wooden school desks from the 50's, a large desk for the teacher, and an old blackboard nailed to the wall. "If you change your mind," Rainwater smiled, "I'll understand. I know this will be a challenge for you. You saw some of the children."

He tried to sound enthusiastic when he spoke. "We have a few who are, at least, somewhat educated. Most are not! I thank the Lord every day for the mercy He has shown me. I was able to go to the university in North Dakota, then I learned Theology at Dallas Seminary, in Texas."

Jennifer looked surprised. "Why did you return to Cedar Ridge, may I ask?"

"I love my people," he answered. "God sent me here and I'll admit it's a bit overwhelming at times; there's so much to do, and so few resources. Thank you for being willing to help, Jennifer. But, like I said, if you have any second thoughts…"

Before he could finish the sentence, she jumped in. "I won't have second thoughts, Mr. Rainwater! You're stuck with me! I will teach these kids, and God will guide me. I will teach them!" She gave Johnny a hug.

"Well," he smiled through tears. "Doggone it! I'm chokin' up now!" He wiped his eyes. "Thank you, thank you!" As Jennifer left John's office that day, she spotted a small boom box on his desk, and next to it, a collection of Creedence Clearwater CDs. It made her laugh.

LATER THAT EVENING, IT WAS TIME FOR ANOTHER MEETING. This time, Johnny Rainwater and Frank from the hardware store joined them. They were all aware that a crisis was coming; only God could give them wisdom to deal with it. They had a small window of time.

Tim and the boys managed to get four restored typewriters with new ribbons installed, and dropped them off at the school. Then Rainwater and Jennifer followed them all back to Tim's cabin. They all settled in the living room together, and even Tim's wife, Nancy, was among them on this night.

Tim Harris sat on a small round area rug in the middle of the floor while the others sat in a circle around him. Tim looked visibly shaken when he finally spoke out. "You all know the book of Hebrews in Chapter 11 describes men and women of faith. In verse 30, it describes some of them as those 'wandering in deserts and mountains and caves, and holes in the ground.' It sounds a bit like us, doesn't it? Well, these people of faith, many of which met their deaths in gruesome ways, endured because of their understanding of a better and new kingdom that God would provide! A kingdom not of this world. If indeed people are being *chipped* by the government, we have a real doosey of a crisis coming our way!

For one thing, there is my sister in Lincoln. She will need to discard her identity and manage to find a way here without being detected. We can't call her, because it is almost certain that the phone is being monitored. She is still a part of Bloomfield's investigation, I'm sure. The deliverance must come from God alone. Sooner or later, Agent Bloomfield will have to assume that all of you must be here, as well, and he will pursue that. I hope we are all in agreement that the Lord is capable of delivering us and equipping us for any work He has for us. I, too, will have to unhook myself from this world. I may need to abandon this house and go to the caves, like in Hebrews 11:38. The weather will hold out for awhile until the brutal winter hits. I know that by faith we must all believe God will bring protection and victory, but my faith is a little shaky right now."

Everyone sat and listened attentively, but no one seemed to want to comment. All those in the room knew of no other way, nor did any of them have a clue to even know where to start!

Finally, Rainwater spoke up. "I guess we all have to play individual parts. Jennifer is welcome to live at the school. If we get any sign that the FBI is snooping around, we have ways to get you all out of sight on Indian land! Even if we have to dress you up and paint your faces and hide you in the tee pee village. I don't know how the government plans to deal with Native Americans, but I'm not real thrilled about the fact that they can change laws and change the rule book at will! So, your guess is as good as mine on that issue."

Then Phil spoke. "It's the unknown that's scary. I don't want to sound lame, but since we are heading into the unknown at this point, we have to assume that God will direct us, and that only He can do that...because nothing is unknown to God. I suggest we get busy preparing the caves and get our Bible-typing project going. I believe the path will open before us, day-by-day and event-by-event!"

This was something they could all agree on. So, it was a done deal for the time. They chatted a bit more about things on the immediate agenda, and then joined hands in prayer. Shortly after the prayer, they were all taken by surprise when Nancy motioned Susan to her side and showed her something in the open Bible that sat on her lap.

Susan looked delighted! "Nancy's got a Word for us, and wants me to read it," she said. Everybody applauded.

She began, "2 Corinthians 4:7-10:
>   *But we have this treasure in earthen vessels, that the surpassing greatness of the power may be of God, and not from ourselves; we are afflicted in every way, but not crushed; perplexed, but not despairing; persecuted, but not forsaken; struck down, but not destroyed; always carrying about in the body, the dying Jesus, that the life of Jesus also may be manifested in our body.'"*

Jennifer smiled at Susan and Nancy, and said, "Thank you for that." She lowered her head. "I guess we have a place to start now. Let's go with it!"

"Yep," Stu agreed. "Each day has enough trouble of its own."

"God knows our needs!" Susan exclaimed. Tim finally smiled for the first time that night.

CHAPTER

Back in Lincoln, Nebraska, Angela Harris wasn't sure what to do. She had heard about the human chipping. No doubt, she would have to go underground very soon.

Agent Bloomfield had her brought in for questioning two days after Patty Miller's arrest. Then again, when she had returned from Rapid City. Bloomfield warned her not to leave town again any time soon without permission, which posed a problem, since she could no longer go anywhere outside Lincoln with any ease. She would also have to avoid Rapid City. Bloomfield knew about her family ties and would be suspicious if she visited her brother at a time like this. It was risky enough that she had been having fellowship with a small group of Christians who lived at a farmhouse 25 miles south of Lincoln. None of them were legal, and none had IDs.

The fellowship group also had the dilemma of never gaining access to a safe Bible. Although Angela was loved and welcome there, she had to dismiss any possibility of moving to the farmhouse, because it would put them in danger.

The question was, how could she come up with a plan to cause a false trail that would lead the FBI to think she went somewhere else, like Canada, for instance while she secretly relocated in Rapid City? This was one of the big reasons that Christians could not risk being chipped! Even if it turned out not to be the Mark of the Beast of the book of Revelation, there was the problem that once chipped, you could no longer discard your ID.

Her thoughts were suddenly interrupted by the doorbell. Every time Angela heard the doorbell, it brought fear.

This time, it was only a mail carrier, wanting her to sign for a package that was sent special delivery. After signing, she received a small box, with a letter. Although regular mail was not always the safest way to stay in touch, it was safer than e-mail. Angela first opened the letter, and started reading.

> *Dearest Angela,*
>
> *It took a long time to locate you. My apologies. I sent this on behalf of Reverend Dennis Taylor, whom you may recall, was a great partner at Lincoln Baptist Church in 2003. As you may also recall, you took him into your own home and helped him with expenses for his return trip to our home church. We were not able to find you until recently, so you are probably not aware that Dennis lost his battle with cancer last year. When he was still in the hospital, shortly before his passing, he made a request to locate you and see that you received his journal as a parting gift. Most of his journal is made up of entries from 1970-1976, when he was attending Bible School in Omaha. He wanted to share those memories with you, and requested personally that you be directed to look at page 40 in particular. We prayed over this mail, that it would reach you unharmed. If you now hold it in your hands, then our prayers have been answered.*
>
> *In Christ, God's Messenger*

Angie carefully unwrapped the journal, and didn't waste any time turning to page 40. Then, she read the entry dated October 19, 1975. She was mesmerized as she read:

Wow, today Doug and I did the strangest thing! We made an old fire extinguisher into a time capsule, and filled it with Bibles. Then we put it in the ground near the ninth hole at Spring Lake Park. It's buried in the middle of a grove of trees about 50 yards from the green. It's crazy! We don't know why we did it! I guess we figured it might be found some day after a nuclear war or something! Well, I'm signing off for today—gotta study.

Angie tucked the journal in her back pocket, and left her ID in her dresser drawer.

She needed to get to the farm right away and talk to the underground Christians. Later, when they all saw the journal, they were astonished!

"Do you think they'd still be there?" one of them asked.

Angela smiled. "Only one way to find out."

Two of the brothers stood quickly. "Let's make a run to Omaha and check this out!"

Then, Mary, one of the sisters placed a hand on Angela's shoulder. "While they're gone, maybe you and I can come up with a plan for you, too; it might be risky, but I think I got an idea how to get you to Rapid City."

Mary and Angela then sat together at the kitchen table. Mary told Angie, "I think I know how we can cause a diversion, so that Bloomfield will think you're either dead, or in Canada."

The two brothers at that time were heading for the shed to get shovels. Angie knew she would be on edge until they returned safely.

Mary went on, "The diversion will be easy, Angie, first you tell Bloomfield you need permission to leave town on business; if he says okay, then you buy a ticket to Alberta, Canada, on Greyhound."

Angela interrupted. "I don't want to go to Canada, Mary!"

"You won't—but your luggage will!" Mary continued, "Now, hear me out! The people at the bus station are usually pretty sloppy, and in a hurry. They tear tickets and cram everyone on the buses quickly. They rarely bother to check names or ticket numbers. They most likely won't know or even care if you boarded or not." Mary then stood up, as she continued talking.

"Bloomfield will probably track you by satellite from your ID card chip. Your signal will show a slow movement toward Canada. After some time goes by and he concludes you are not returning, he'll think you fled! He'll figure two things. One, that you signed papers to become a citizen of Canada and voided your U.S. ID; or two, you destroyed your U.S. card and went into hiding illegally. By then, you'll be in Rapid City. We have an unregistered vehicle and a couple of us can get you there somehow. That's the risky part; but I believe God will protect us. I believe God will make a way so that we won't encounter any cops or get scanned. That's the plan!"

Angela slumped back in her chair. "Brilliant!" she shouted. "Let's do it!"

AT THE CEDAR RIDGE RESERVATION, the school room behind Rainwater's office proved to be a good place to have a typing marathon. Jennifer, Stu, Todd, and Phillip were all good typists. John Rainwater had an old overhead projector in the storeroom. They managed to shine the Scriptures large and clear from Tim's "New American Standard Bible" on the wall of the school room. They figured if they put in enough hours per day, they could have copies of the New Testament by the end of the week.

Susan mostly stayed at Tim's cabin and cared for his wife, Nancy. Tim and Frank worked together to locate more supplies for the caves—canned food, bottled water, medicines, blankets, and spare batteries among many other items. Most of the supplies were stored at the cabin for now. The main priority was to get finished copies of the Scriptures.

Sheriff Gabe Lewis also stopped in one night to give them an update on Bloomfield. Bloomfield had contacted him again, and Gabe had done his best to try and assure him that he had seen nothing unusual at the Harris residence. That was true, because in Gabe's mind, nothing WAS unusual. Gabe also got the news that Patty Miller was still in solitary confinement, until her execution date.

In Lincoln, Nebraska, Angela was getting a bit nervous on the night the brothers left for Omaha on their Bible hunt. She waited in fear for their return. It was shortly after midnight when they finally did return, dragging a rusted, round cylinder crusted with dirt into the house. During the digging, they did not need to worry so much about being spotted after dark. What took the most time was finding the exact burial spot. They were laughing about the fact that the land space near the trees was full of so many holes it resembled a cribbage board, but they eventually found the thing!

It was a beautiful sight when they finally removed the cap and spilled out the contents on the farm house floor. It contained 12 pocket size New Testaments. Six of them were King James Version, six New American Standard. There were also three complete Bibles—two N.A.S.B., and the third was a King James Version. They were all in perfect condition.

After a period of thanks and celebration, Mary filled everybody in on the plan for Angela's return to South Dakota. They all agreed that the plan would work! They would proceed with it first thing the next day. Angela would need to meet with Bloomfield and tie up that end in the morning, and if all went well, they would proceed from there.

Angela began to pray silently in her heart. "Thank you, Lord, for providing your Word to us in the fellowship. The travel plans, I leave in Your power—show me the best way. Show me Your way, Lord Jesus." Angela knew that possible dangers were ahead. She hoped in her heart that God had a safer way in His plan for her to reach Rapid City. She had peace about the luggage being sent to Canada—but had serious doubts about traveling in an unregistered vehicle.

DAY OF RESISTANCE

PART TWO: The Resistance

AGENT BLOOMFIELD OF THE FBI worked out of the Omaha office. He was in charge over most of the counties in the region, from Omaha to Lincoln, and some counties extending to Grand Island. His job was very specific. He specialized in bringing to justice all who were suspected of being involved with what he referred to as "The Resistance." The reason that Christians such as Patty Miller were included in this category went back a few years.

In the 1980s and 90s, 12-step programs started to become very popular as the answer to alcoholism and other addiction issues. The method was used readily in treatment centers and anonymous programs. Originally, the 12 steps had a lot of legitimacy, and were used very successfully in recovery; however, when it came down to the existence of God, it taught a form of universalism.

God was not referred to as the God of the Jews, or as the one who appeared to humanity in the form of Jesus Christ, but was referred to as "The Higher Power" and also, "God as we understood Him."

As the "higher power" teaching became more and more popular, many people became less tolerant of the "God of the Bible." In the 12-step teachings, God no longer had a specific identity. People in the programs assigned him a personal identity, according to everyone's individual viewpoint. People got comfortable with the idea of viewing God in their own way. Also, this was highly embraced, because the concept was not offensive to others.

As time went on, the universal idea spread outside the 12-step programs into social circles and even into many of the churches. As it spread, more intolerance of the "God of the Bible" grew also.

In no time at all, cases started appearing before the Supreme Court by people who believed that traditional Christian teaching was violating their rights.

These included teachings such as what is included in Romans 1, which declares that homosexuality is a sin and an unnatural act against the will and plan of God. Furthermore, the Bible taught that "All have sinned and fall short of God's standards," causing all of the human race to be separated from God and spiritually dead, placing all people under the sentence of death and hell. This judgement was remedied only by faith and trust in Jesus Christ for forgiveness and redemption. Only Jesus, and Jesus alone, could bring rebirth to a sinner, resulting in eternal life, because only He pleased the Father and resurrected from the dead.

Those of the Islamic faith, especially, were gravely offended by these teachings, and claimed it was a blasphemy!

To clear up this whole religious mess, the "Federal Church Act" was established and declared as law! All churches were to register with the government and comply with the teachings of universalism. A panel of scholars was brought together to combine the teachings of all major religions to agree with a common thought that pleased almost everyone. A text was created called "The Common Bible." This became the approved textbook that all registered churches were required to use...and all registered religious organizations were closely monitored by law enforcement. Those who chose to resist the order, and followed God independently (such as Patty Miller) were labeled as part of "The Resistance."

Many Christians like Patty, who studied the original Old and New Testaments and the foundational teachings concerning Jesus as the Christ, were soon discovered by the FBI. This was due to computer chipping in the pages of the Bibles which allowed tracking. Plus, the authorities tapped into Internet postings and e-mails. Those of Patty's friends who discovered this, began to use only "safe" Bibles; they were a little harder to trace.

Lawrence Bloomfield pursued these people. Not just because of their personal belief in Jesus, but because *that, in itself, was not unlawful.* It had become a criminal offense when it was taught to others outside the lawful confines of "The Church Act."

Most of them were sentenced to execution if they chose not to cooperate. Many were considered to be *chronically resistant to rehabilitation,* and had to be eliminated, "lest they become a constant menace to society." They also had to be stopped in order that the "Resistance" would not rapidly grow in numbers. Bloomfield had already come to the conclusion the year before, that the "Resistance" was already becoming too powerful.

So, Bloomfield did his research. He monitored Angela Harris, not realizing that it was only her luggage on the way to Canada. He also checked her bank records, which verified the purchase of a ticket to Calgary, Alberta.

Bloomfield had hoped the signal from her ID card would lead to Rapid City, and was surprised that the signal indicated that she really went to Canada, where he had no jurisdiction. Bloomfield had allowed the trip, with the belief that she would change directions, and head for South Dakota.

He had even called the head of the Sheriff's Department in Rapid City, Gabe Lewis, who had no knowledge of Angela's presence. Sheriff Lewis had an impeccable record in law enforcement; so Bloomfield had no cause to doubt his story. This had been a long week for Agent Bloomfield, and it was only the beginning.

ANGELA FOUND OUT VERY QUICKLY how different things would be, living as a member of "The Resistance" with no ID or bankcard. She was no longer given the ability to purchase goods. She learned from the members of the farmhouse fellowship what good old-fashioned trading was all about.

The fellowship was fortunate for the time being. The Lord had led them to an elderly couple about a mile down the road. An elderly black couple, named Joe and Margaret Freeman.

The Freemans were born-again believers that still had possession of their IDs—although, soon that would change. The brothers and sisters of the fellowship traded with them often for things that needed to be purchased with a bankcard...like gas, food, and medicine. Much of the time, the Freemans gave charity because many items they took in trade from the fellowship, they really didn't need.

Now, the fellowship finally had something of great value to offer. The Freemans had been longing for a Bible. When Angela and Mary showed up at their door with a slim leather bound New American Standard Bible, Joe Freeman's eyes nearly bulged out of his head. A mint condition safe Bible from 1975! It was an incredible gift.

After spending a long time learning about the circumstances surrounding Angela, they listened to Mary's pitch. It was simple. The old 1998 Chevy Blazer that the fellowship owned was an unregistered vehicle—the very one they planned to use to transport Angela to Rapid City.

All that Mary was asking to exchange for the Bible was to have the vehicle filled with gas, plus she needed an extra 5-gallon can to take with them.

Joe and Margaret asked them to sit a moment. "We've got a better idea," Joe said. "Look, you are taking a big risk to go that far in an illegal car, especially when you are all illegals yourselves!" He looked toward his wife. "Hon, tell 'em what we got planned, darlin'."

Margaret had such a warm beautiful smile. "Well we was thinkin' of doin' one more thing before we leave this old life behind, before gettin' rid of our cards, that is. We got a nice RV parked in the barn, and we've always wanted to take a nice trip to the Black Hills, and see Mount Rushmore. So what do you say we all go together on this one? It will be the last legal vacation we'll have!"

Angela lost control of her emotions and began to cry. "You'd do that for me? Really?"

"Well," Joe answered calmly, "we've been wantin' to go for a long time; now God has given us a reason to go!"

Mary returned to the farmhouse with Angela, to help her pack. Mary decided to stay in Nebraska with the other believers. As the Freemans were beginning to collect the belongings they needed for the trip, Joe picked up the new Bible and opened it to the Gospel of John, where Jesus was saying to His disciples, "Greater love has no man than this. That a man lay down his life for his friends." Then he and his wife joined hands and thanked God together. Following this last vacation together, they would be discarding their old life—they would become strangers to the world, renegades, members of "The Resistance."

17
CHAPTER

"This rock looks like a good place to sit a spell." Tim was stressed. He and Frank had been in the caves most of the day. They had discovered numerous numbers of storage spaces, and they were putting them to good use with canned goods, books, batteries, and other items they had managed to glean from Frank's store. For the last few days, Tim had been concerned about his sister, Angela. "Frank, I can't imagine how she'll find a way to get here undetected—although the Lord keeps giving me peace about it."

Frank nodded his head as if in agreement. "She is very resourceful, Tim. She'll be here, I know she will, So, not to worry, Reverend."

It felt good to sit and take a break. Tim guzzled down some fresh water from the ice cooler. "So, what's up in the news, Frank?" he asked.

Frank appeared worried. "Well, Tim, there was a terrorist attack in Chicago this morning. A synagogue bombing. A bunch of kids and a Rabbi were killed! The kids were taking a class to get ready for their bar mitzvahs, the only ones in the building at that time, I guess. Well they're all dead now. They say on the news that five different countries in the Middle East now have the bomb!"

Phil moaned and gave a sour laugh. "We should have made a move years ago, Frank, but as you know, prophecy will be fulfilled."

Frank looked toward the floor of the cave. "They closed the Wyoming border, Tim—nobody gets in or out. It's some kind of nasty virus that's killing people by the hundreds."

Tim shook his head. "Man, it seems so strange to be running around like fugitives, just because we know Jesus, and want to read the Bible, ain't it, Frank? I always knew the time was coming, but it seemed so much like a storybook. Not really real! Now that it's here, it is still hard to fathom. 'We are raised up and seated with Christ in the heavenly places,' is what Paul wrote in Ephesians. God will call us out to spread His Word more boldly once He has tested us and made us ready. We will need to be willing to die, Frank!"

This statement appeared to make Frank's body jerk, as though he got punched in the gut. He responded by quickly changing the subject. "Well Tim, the sun's goin' down. I guess we'd better be heading out to the school to pick up Jennifer. Hey, where are the boys?"

"Oh, they're still in the other cave," Tim answered. "I'll whistle for 'em, and we'll get goin,' I guess."

Jennifer had spent most of her day getting to know the kids who showed up for school. Only six of them. Five of them were eight to ten years of age—three boys, and two girls. The sixth student was 12-years-old. His name was Billy Whitebird. Billy was the one that Jennifer was most concerned with. He seemed overly quiet and withdrawn. He had amazing skills at drawing pictures. He could pencil-draw with skilled detail, but the pictures were quite bizarre and disturbing! One picture was of his father brandishing a knife with one hand, and holding a whiskey bottle in the other. Billy drew atomic bomb explosions, tornadoes, and bleeding men pelted with bullet wounds. In yet another drawing, a field full of dead blackbirds. Jennifer tried many different tactics in order to attempt communication with Billy, but all he would do was stare at the floor in silence. Johnny Rainwater knew very little about the boy, and could not shed any light on the issue.

Rainwater and Jennifer, despite the drama, seemed to be hitting it off quite well. They were beginning to like each other as more than just friends.

Susan, at this time, continued to read the Scripture to Tim's wife, Nancy. Every day, little-by-little, Nancy seemed to be doing better and finding more ways to cope with her disability.

Todd, Phil, and Stuart spend most of their days helping with the caves. The last that they head from Sheriff Gabe concerning Patty Miller was that she was still waiting for her execution date. Gabe had called the Sheriff's office in Scottsbluff, Nebraska, and spoke with Sheriff Sebastian Connolly, head of the Scottsbluff Sheriff department. Connolly informed him that there was little or nothing he could do for those already incarcerated at the prison. Connolly mostly concentrated on protecting the members of his own community, to try and prevent troublemakers from being sent there in the first place. Connolly was a born-again believer, who owned a couple of safe Bibles and conducted a secret home Bible study.

The believers in Rapid City met at Tim's after the long day's end and prayed over everything. They got into the Word together and studied Scriptures about the work of the Holy Spirit.

Jennifer had a restless sleep that night. She could not get Billy Whitebird out of her mind. She was still disturbed about his drawings. On those rare occasions when Billy would speak, it was always with a one word reply. When she pointed to the drawing of his day, "What is this one, Billy?"

He responded with the word, "Fear." With the tornado, he answered, "Escape," with the atomic bomb, "London," with the dead birds, "Iowa." Then he would stare at the floor for another hour. When Jennifer finally pointed to the drawing of the men ridden with bullets, Billy finally spoke two words—"The Wall."

BOTH ANGELA AND THE FREEMANS were enjoying the trip to South Dakota. They stopped overnight in a campground near Yankton on the first night. It was the first time in about 10 years that Angela was able to forget the pressures of the world and enjoy a peaceful, quiet night.

They all had wonderful fellowship while sitting comfortably on lawn chairs outside the RV. The moon and stars cast a mild halo of light. Margaret made some popcorn that they indulged in, as they sat among the stars talking about the beauty of Jesus and the awesome presence of God. When they went to sleep that night, it was as if Jesus Himself gently tucked them in.

When the early dawn finally came, they were anxious to be on the road. To save some time, they all had a quick breakfast at a roadside café right outside the town of Yankton. It would be easy to reach Rapid City by nightfall.

"You can drop me off right here." Angela smiled a few hours later. The RV was parked right in front of the Golden 8 Cinema at the Rapid City shopping mall. "I just need to use your cell phone for a sec, then we'll say our goodbyes." Joe handed his cell phone to Angela and she quickly dialed the number at Frank's store.
Frank answered as usual, "Yep."

"Frank, it's me!"

"Oh, yeah, Sweetheart, I know the voice—where you at, darlin'?" he asked.

"At Golden 8 Cinema, Frank. Can you come get me?"

"On my way," Frank answered with a tone of both excitement and fear. When they disconnected the call, Angela was relieved that Frank had the wisdom not to say her name while on the call. In reality, it probably made no difference, but in these days, one could never be too careful.

Joe looked at Angela and forced a weak smile. "God be with you, sister. We will really miss you, it's been a wonderful time."

Margaret then added, "And thank you so much for the Bible—it means more than you can imagine, my dear."

"And thank you," Angela responded. "Thank you for getting me here safely, and enjoy Mt. Rushmore—it's awesome!"

Margaret then put her arm around Angela. "Let's pray real quick, okay?"

Joe placed a hand on Angie's shoulder and they prayed over her. "Lord, we ask your protection and blessing on our sister, that You will guide her in all of Your ways and renew her every day with courage and faith to follow You closely—we ask it in Jesus name, and thank you for hearing our prayer."

They all embraced one final time. The RV remained parked there till

Frank arrived. Angela smiled and waved at the Freemans as Frank's truck pulled onto the exit road.

AGENT BLOOMFIELD WAS HAVING his 10:00 p.m. cup of coffee back in Omaha. He was parked at his office desk, chatting with Agent Lee Mattson, his friend and right-hand man in the Department.

"I'm not satisfied!" Bloomfield barked. "The more I think about it, I'm not sure I can trust that sheriff in Rapid City. These kids and Tim's sister are up to something. Lee, you might remember that this Reverend Harris got into some trouble a while back by making radical statements about God and religion. The Church Act law was not in place then, so he really couldn't get busted for it. Why am I to assume that Reverend Harris is no longer involved in The Resistance? Maybe he and that Sheriff Gabe character are in cahoots!"

Lee pulled his chair closer to Bloomfield's desk. "So, what do you intend to do, Larry?" he asked.

Bloomfield smiled. "I'm gonna send an agent undercover!" He then leaned back in his chair. "It took some thinking, but I finally came up with a plan. A reporter—a news reporter who wants to interview Harris for a documentary! This reporter with his camera will tweak Harris' ego with his interest in the Reverend's background, and his opinion on The Church Act, and so on."

Lee scratched his chin. "Do you think he'll fall for it?"

"Sure," Bloomfield bellowed. "He's the type of guy who'd never pass up an opportunity like that! He loves to give his opinions publicly. That's what got him into trouble in the first place. But now that he's no longer a registered minister, he can pretty much say what he wishes, without repercussions!"

Lee shied away from Bloomfield's desk. "You got anyone in mind to go undercover?" he asked, knowing that it was probably him.

Bloomfield laughed and pointed his finger at Lee. Lee stood as if to make a speech. "So, I'm going to be 'Lee Matson, mild mannered reporter.' Should I take Lois Lane and Jimmy Olsen with me?"

"This isn't a joke, Lee!" Bloomfield shouted.

"Ok," Lee agreed. "I do know some things about sound equipment and video cameras. I guess I could sound professional and play it up. I'll just need to look real. I'll need a TV van with a convincing logo—AND a convincing ID card."

Bloomfield stood up from his chair, went to the west wall of his office, and opened a panel door. He grabbed two shot glasses and his favorite bottle of 30-year-old bourbon, and poured the shots when he returned to the desk. "Ok," he smiled. "Let's have a drink and figure out how to nail these bums."

As the brothers and sisters gathered together at Tim's cabin, along with John Rainwater they had a very nice homecoming celebration for Angela. Besides the ice cream and cake, they enjoyed loving fellowship, prayer, and reading from God's Word.

They all experienced some conviction from a passage that Phil read from 1 Thessalonians 4:9-12:

> *"Now as to the love of the brethren, you have no need for anyone to write to you, for you yourselves are taught by God to love one another; for indeed you do practice it toward all the brethren who are in all Macedonia. But we urge you, brethren, to excel still more, and to make it your ambition to lead a quiet life and attend to your own business and work with your hands just as we commanded you; so that you may behave properly toward outsiders and not be in any need."*

Tim considered this reading from Scripture as a confirmation. For the last couple of days, Tim had had much conversation with Rainwater. It was pretty much decided that when Tim disposed of his ID card, and in order to avoid being chipped, he would have to move to Indian land and live among the Native Americans.

So far, Johnny Rainwater had not received any indication or notice from the federal government to the effect that Cedar Ridge would be expected to participate in any new legislation. As far as Rainwater knew, it would be business as usual under Indian law.

Of course, he and Tim both knew that it could all change overnight! After reading from 1 Thessalonians, they all believed that God was leading them to keep a quiet and low profile, unless circumstances warranted otherwise; also to trust the Lord for all of their needs.

For the last ten years, the government had been funding Cedar Ridge with taxpayer money, but that could easily change as well. This was a test of faith many of the Indian reservations faced time and time again.

Johnny shared some good thoughts on the subject. "The Lord taught us that when we pray," he said, "that we go into our private room and close the door, in order to pray to our Heavenly Father in secret. When He sees our secret prayers, He will reward us openly. If we pray to Him, and Him only, we will know the answer comes from God. Private prayer manipulates no one."

Then Stu shared, "And that is a hard thing. It is difficult to believe God for things that are unseen. We must completely give up the control of our lives, and our will to the Lord. I don't know that any of us have reached that point in our faith completely, but I know that God can give us that ability."

Then Stu read another passage from 1 Thessalonians 5:23-24:
"Now may the God of peace Himself sanctify you entirely; and may your spirit and soul and body be preserved

complete, without blame at the coming of our Lord Jesus Christ. Faithful is He who calls you, and He also will bring it to pass."

Tim Harris did not know yet that in a few short days he would be approached by an imposter posing as a news reporter—although, it had been revealed to Jennifer by Billy Whitebird.

Earlier that day, as Jennifer sat with the children in her classroom, Billy drew a new picture. A man with a camera displaying a shy, devilish grin! When she asked Billy about the picture, he said the word, "Imposter." Jennifer had not yet told Tim, but she soon would. She knew it had something to do with the near future, just like Billy's other drawings.

Back in Bloomfield's world in Nebraska, the FBI had already looked into a report of a cult group of illegals outside of Lincoln. The six worshippers they found at the farmhouse were hauled away and jailed, although Bloomfield could get no information from them about Angela Harris or any of Patty Miller's friends.

When the Freemans returned to Lincoln in their RV, they were still legal, but did not intend to stay that way for long. They dropped by the farmhouse, and were surprised to find it empty.

"What do you say we ditch our IDs here in Lincoln, and hightail it back to Rapid City?" Joe asked his wife.

Joe's wife, Margaret, was aware that the empty farmhouse meant danger, and she answered, saying, "Yes, Joe, let's go camping again, by faith, and this time, we don't ever come back!"

In the town of Scottsbluff, Nebraska, Patty Miller sat alone in her prison cell, as July turned to August. She was due for execution on August 31.

LEE MATTSON ARRIVED THREE DAYS LATER. He was driving a white van with logo on the side reading in big bold letters "KVXN NEWS—WE ARE IN THE KNOW!" Then, under that in smaller letters, "A leader in national news information." Lee slowly pulled up to a parking space in front of Quick Lunch Soup and Sandwiches, located right next door to Frank's Hardware. Before exiting the van to feed his ravaging hunger and indulge in several cups of coffee, he rolled down the driver's side window and shot a few pictures of Main Street on his cell phone camera. He wanted to document the entire trip. He would later upload all of the pictures so that Bloomfield, back in Omaha, would be able to view them. Lee also figured he would inquire about the whereabouts of Timothy Harris, while inside Quick Lunch. Once he entered, the small café caught his attention right away. It was all made up in 1950s décor. As Lee sat down for coffee, he noticed a Wurlitzer Jukebox filled with old 45 r.p.m. records of Elvis, The Everly Brothers, Buddy Holly, and other famed rockers from the 50s. At the time, it was blaring "Splish Splash" by Bobby Darin.

Lee was instantly in love with the town, yet he knew that this small community which seemed to have no name, held mysteries.

He finally asked the waitress, when things got quieter, if she knew of Reverend Harris.

"He lives in a cabin. You just take Rural Route 29 straight west a couple miles. You can't miss it because it's the only cabin with three floors," she said.

"Thanks," Lee nodded.

"So what brings you here?" the waitress asked.

"I'm with KVXN News, I'm here to do a story on Reverend Harris." He reached in his back pocket to pull out his wallet.

"Good luck with that!" The waitress smiled. "He's a pretty private kind of guy."

Lee tanked up on some more coffee and finished his lunch, then left the waitress a generous tip, thanking her again. He decided to check into a small Motel 6 he spotted by the roadside, to get cleaned up before going to Tim's cabin. He finally settled into his room and plugged his cell phone into his laptop computer, and noticed that three people showed up in one of the pictures. They were seated together on a bench that was located in the middle of the town square.

He zoomed in and enlarged it. He was shocked by what he saw. Lee quickly entered the data into the laptop and frantically dialed Bloomfield's number in Omaha.

"Bloomfield!" The voice boomed on the third ring.

"Hey, it's Lee! Get your computer up on the personal file! I've got one hell of a picture to send. You ain't gonna believe this, Lawrence!"

After a moment of silence, Bloomfield spoke. "Ok, I see it. Wow!

You're not kidding, Lee!"

"Do you see what I see?" Lee asked.

"Yep," Bloomfield sounded excited. "It definitely looks like Angie Harris. The blonde gal sitting with her looks like one of Patty Miller's cultist friends! I think her name's Jennifer, if I remember correctly. I don't know the third one. Looks like some longhaired Indian from the reservation, to me."

"So, what now?" Lee asked.

Bloomfield answered, "This definitely changes the plan, now that we got proof that the Harris lady never went to Canada after all. My hunch proved to be right all along." Bloomfield paused for a moment. "Okay, Lee, I'll tell you what. Just hang tight and stay low for now. I'll catch the next flight to Rapid City. I'll call you when I get there, and then we'll decide what to do next. My guess is that good ol' Sheriff Gabe knew all along. We're gonna bust these turkeys! All of 'em!" Then Bloomfield disconnected.

While all of this was transpiring, the waitress from Quick Lunch ran next door to Frank's Hardware and told Frank that a news guy was looking for Tim Harris. Whether right or wrong, she'd lied to Lee about the cabin location in order to buy time. Just two days prior to Lee's arrival, she and others in the community were warned to look out for an Imposter posing as a news reporter!

They were warned about the FBI investigating Angela and Tim's step-son, Stu. Jennifer never explained the details about Billy Whitebird's pictures. That would sound farfetched. The one thing the waitress didn't know was that Lee had taken that photo. Frank quickly jumped into his truck and headed toward Tim's place. Finally, everyone was rounded up to meet at the school house. They had to be sure they were on Indian land immediately. Rainwater already had planned to have an armed welcoming committee if any strangers attempted to enter Cedar Ridge.

AGENT BLOOMFIELD FINALLY ARRIVED at the airport in Rapid City at 6:00 that evening. He rented a car and drove to the motel where Agent Mattson was staying. Before trying to locate Tim Harris, they decided to drive back to Rapid City and confront Sheriff Gabe Lewis. Bloomfield wasn't happy when he entered the downtown office of the Sheriff's Department. Bloomfield slammed a printout of Lee's photo on Gabe's desk. "Who do you see in this picture, Sheriff?!" he roared. "C'mon, take a good look! Do you not recognize Angela Harris?" Bloomfield's face was beginning to turn red. "This was only taken just yesterday, Gabe! You see that young girl with her? She's one of Patty Miller's cult members!"

Sheriff Lewis shook his head. "I don't know the girl with her, but, yes, that is Angela Harris. So why is that so unusual? She visits her brother from time to time."

Bloomfield's temper was still rising. "What is unusual, you idiot, is that she led us to believe she went to Canada! She got rid of her ID card, disappeared, and lied to the FBI after being told to stay in town for interrogation!"

Bloomfield was pacing the floor. "I consider her a fugitive."

Sheriff Lewis began to sweat and appeared nervous.

"Gabe? This is Agent Lee Mattson. I figure the three of us should go to the Harris residence right now and clear up this mess! Do you agree?"

Gabe reluctantly grabbed his hat off of his desk. He followed Mattson and Bloomfield out the door. Gabe informed his desk clerk that he would be gone for the rest of the evening.

When they were about to get into Bloomfield's rental car, Agent Mattson pointed a gun in Gabe's face. "You need to surrender your firearm now!" he ordered.

The Sheriff's hand was shaking as he gave up his weapon, and they all proceeded in the car together, to drive to Tim's cabin.

"So, I'm a suspect?" Gabe asked.

"What do YOU think?" Bloomfield said sarcastically, as he put Gabe in handcuffs. "We believe Reverend Harris is housing at least five fugitives, and you told me on the phone two weeks ago that nothing unusual was going on there!"

Gabe remained silent while Bloomfield ranted. "I also checked phone records and found out you made a call to Sheriff Connolly in Scottsbluff, Nebraska. I called him myself and was told you called to check on the status of a death row prisoner. Patty Miller, perhaps?" Bloomfield's eyebrows raised. "Well, Connolly wasn't very talkative, so I'll need you to fill in the blanks!"

Gabe still did not speak, except to indicate that they were approaching the Harris property. They parked in front of the cabin. They exited the car, but when they reached Tim's front door, they found the cabin dark and empty.

Shortly after Frank got the message from the Quick Lunch, the waitress, Susan, and Tim's wife Nancy, left the house and rode with Frank to Cedar Ridge.

Tim and the boys were found milling about, near the caves. Jennifer and Angela were already at the school. Rainwater was in his office drinking coffee. When he heard the story, he called Gabe's office and was informed by the desk clerk that Sheriff Lewis had left for the night, being escorted by two men in suits.

"Bloomfield's in town," Rainwater said to the others. He stood from the chair and walked over to the schoolroom door. "Here's what we'll do," he continued. "Everyone except Tim, I want you all to take the back door exit in the schoolroom. Stu will show you the trail in the back of the building. It leads to the Tee Pee Village. I'll call Chief Blackbear right now. He'll get you out of sight! Nancy? I guess it is best you stay here with your husband after all. It's kind of a long walk. This is just a precaution—so don't freak out on me. The chances are that Bloomfield won't even get beyond the front gate!"

Gabe gave directions for Bloomfield to drive to Cedar Ridge. On the main road leading to the front gate, their path was blocked by six Indians with rifles. One of them called Rainwater's office. "We got a problem, John. Bloomfield is here along with Gabe Lewis. It appears that Gabe is in custody, because they've got him cuffed!"

There was silence for a moment, then Rainwater finally answered. "Ok, go ahead and disarm them, and tell them to free Gabe. Then, bring them to me!"

The same Indian pointed his rifle toward the agents. "You heard the speakerphone, Mr. FBI man. Set your firearms on the ground, now!"

"And if I don't?" Bloomfield shouted. The Indian looked solemn as he eyed Bloomfield.

"You are on Indian land, Sir! You have no jurisdiction here! There are six of us and two of you. If you don't give up your weapons and come with us, we will have to take action. And keep this in mind, Bloomfield, look around you. Do you see all of the rocks, hills and valleys surrounding us? If your friends come looking for you, they will never find you, OR your dead body! So, I think you'd better come with us right now!"

Bloomfield became shaken and motioned for Agent Mattson to remove Gabe's handcuffs. They handed over their police revolvers and proceeded to follow the six guards to Rainwater's office.

JUST OUTSIDE LINCOLN, NEBRASKA, Mary from the farmhouse fellowship sat alone in the darkness of the fruit cellar located on the property. It was dark, moldy and damp. She had been there for how many hours? She didn't really know! Mary not only felt alone, but ashamed.

Early that afternoon she had gone for a long walk to spend some time alone in prayer. After a lengthy stroll in the fields, she began to return to the house, and just as she reached the backyard where the cellar was located, she saw four police cars pull up to the house. She was stricken with fear and fled into the cellar to hide. She could hear the voices of her friends as they were being taken away. Now, several hours had passed. Mary knew that in reality she was not alone, because the Lord was with her. The fellowship group had also stored the Bibles in the cellar, so she had access to His Word, as well.

Mary felt around in the dark until she found the camping flashlight. Thank the Lord the batteries were still good. Now that she could see, she also found the Bibles. It was amazing to her that she spent those long hours in darkness before finally discovering light! She had been crying out to God in prayer during that time. "Please forgive my fear and lack of faith, Dear Lord." Now that she could see, she opened one of the Bibles and shone the flashlight upon its precious words. She had opened it to 1 Peter 1:3:

> *"Blessed be the God and Father of our Lord Jesus Christ, who according to His great mercy has caused us to be born again to a living hope through the resurrection of Christ from the dead, to obtain an inheritance which is imperishable and undefiled and will not fade away, reserved in heaven for you, who are protected by the power of God through faith for a salvation ready to be revealed in the last time. In this you greatly rejoice, even though now for a little while, if necessary you have been distressed by various trials, that the proof of your faith, being more precious than gold which is perishable, even though tested by fire, may be found to result in praise and glory and honor at the revelation of Jesus Christ; and though you have not seen Him, you love Him, and though you do not see Him now, but believe in Him, you greatly rejoice with joy inexpressible and full of glory, obtaining as the outcome of your faith the salvation of your souls."*

Mary read this and cried out to God again. "Reveal your will to me, Father. Why was I spared? Deliver me and show me where to go, God, and give me the strength to follow."

All of this time, Mary had been so paralyzed with fear that she had dared not emerge from the cellar. She was still afraid, even now, to leave her hiding place, but suddenly the cellar door flew open!

"Is anyone down there? Can you hear me?"

"Oh, my Lord, Joe!" She cried as she recognized the voice of Joe Freeman. She got to her feet and stumbled up the stairs and into his arms. "Joe! Thank God it's really you!" She could not stop crying and holding on to him.

"Yes, yes," he answered while comforting her. "It's me, alright. Margaret and I just got back today and found the place empty, but right before we left, God put a conviction on our hearts to look around the place first!"

Mary spoke through her tears. "The cops came, Joe. They took everyone away except me."

"Then we better get outta here," Joe responded.

Margaret looked down into the cellar from the doorway. "C'mon, honey you can come along with us. We're gonna blow this town. Don't know where we're goin,' but we sure can't stay around here!"

Mary took one more trip down in the cellar to get the Bibles, handed some of them to Margaret, and they all quickly ran for the RV. Soon, they were fishtailing down the dirt driveway to the main highway, leaving a cloud of dust behind.

CHAPTER

AGENT BLOOMFIELD, ALONG WITH AGENT MATTSON and Sheriff
Gabe Lewis were escorted to John Rainwater's office. Rainwater
sat at his desk and on a chair in the corner also sat Tim Harris.

Once they were all seated, the six escorts left the room. Tim gave
Bloomfield a hard stare. "Ok, now that we are finally here, face-
to-face...what is it that you came all this way to find, Lawrence?"
Tim asked.

Bloomfield barked his answer. "You already know that, Reverend!
You have been giving shelter and protection to five fugitives—Stu
Watson, Jennifer Houston, Susan Miller, Todd Mason, and Phillip
Jackson. Is that true?"

Tim chuckled at this. "Well, I see you've done your homework,
Bloomfield, but actually, there are six. You forgot my sister,
Angela, and they are not in protective custody. They are all here
as guests of the community. So what is it you want with them?"

Bloomfield's face began to turn red with anger. "You know damn
well what I want, Reverend! I'm here to bring them in—they are all
under arrest for disregarding registration laws, for being members
of an anti-government cult, and for teaching anti-government
propaganda with intention to recruit others!"

"They are now on reservation land!" Tim countered. Then Tim's face grew calm with what appeared to be a gentle look of love and compassion.

"Look, Bloomfield, please don't misunderstand me. We are a peaceful people in this community. We are not anti-government terrorists. These college kids want to believe the original Bible, they want to follow Jesus, and know that their sins are forgiven. That's all."

Tim held his hands out in front of him as if in an appeal. "They want to love one another and also love others. They believe in sharing God's love, because God loves THEM. You talk about Jennifer as if she were an enemy of the State. She is working here, free of charge, as a teacher for the children here at Cedar Ridge. Do you honestly want to arrest these kids and possibly send them to their deaths, because of what they believe?"

"I have to follow procedure!" Bloomfield barked.

Then Rainwater spoke. "We understand that, Sir, but the reality is that you have no jurisdiction on Indian land, plus you are outnumbered, because most of this whole community is made up of Christians."

Bloomfield scratched his head and began to pace. "Why is it so hard for you Christians to understand? All you have to do is comply with the law. It's so simple! You have the right to run a church legally, if you just cooperate with The Federal Church Act.'"

Tim Harris then stood up in alarm. "That's the whole point! How can we comply with a system that is against the teachings of our

Savior Jesus Christ?! He taught us He was the Way, the Truth, and the Life, and that He is the only one that God sent into the world for our salvation. These young folks are not trying to defy the country, they simply believe what Jesus taught. And besides that, I don't see how they have done any harm to anyone. It is YOU who wants to do harm!"

Bloomfield remained silent as Rainwater also spoke. "Besides what Tim just told you, the Truth still stands. We Native Americans are under our own government here at Cedar Ridge! As long as these people live on our land, they have the freedom to follow their faith!"

"So, what do you propose?" Bloomfield finally asked.

Rainwater gave him a hard look. "We would hope you will have the sense to leave this area and return to Nebraska, where you belong! You really have no place here, unless, of course, you decide to join us and believe in the Lord Jesus for your salvation."

Bloomfield looked like a pressure cooker ready to blow at any minute after hearing this statement. "Don't insult me!" he screamed. "I will get the proper orders to arrest these people! Do you think I won't?"

"Yes," Rainwater answered. "I think you won't! Because, under our laws here, if I think YOU are detrimental to the community's best interests, it is YOU who will be arrested, and YOU who will be detained! As a last resort, I can even shoot you if I have to!" Rainwater paused a moment to let it sink in, then continued. "With this in mind, I think it's best that you return to Omaha and forget about the people here. The people of this community are guilty of nothing and have the right to be left alone! If you return and try anything to hurt these people or pose a threat to us, you will have a war on your hands. Believe me, the potential of bloodshed is not worth the risk over some innocent college kids who want to follow Jesus. Make sense?" Rainwater raised his voice another notch. "YOU WILL LEAVE!"

Bloomfield looked defeated and resigned at this. "Alright, we're gone tomorrow morning, if you insist! But you will not see the last of me, because I WILL seek legal means to bring justice on this haven of yours!"

Bloomfield then grabbed Sheriff Lewis by the arm and yanked him violently forward, so that he banged into Rainwater's desk. "You can keep this traitor! We will be back for a visit very soon, Big Chief!"

"Good-bye, Bloomfield," Rainwater said coldly. "The escorts will return your weapons at the gate when you leave, but let me warn you, Bloomfield—don't test me!"

Bloomfield was escorted out as soon as the guards returned. As he went through the doorway, he turned once more toward Rainwater and Tim. "And don't test ME, Hotshot! I'll see you soon, 'Big Chief'!"

Rainwater smiled. "Jesus lives, Bloomfield. Jesus lives."

25

CHAPTER

THE FREEMANS, WITH SISTER MARY IN TOW, drove the RV straight east through Omaha and over the bridge into Council Bluffs, Iowa. "I'm feelin' like we should take the long way," Joe said. "I figure we head north to Sioux City, and that's where we fill up the tank and gas cans. We'll ditch our ID cards and cellphones, then cross over into South Dakota, and head straight for Rapid City."

"Sounds like a plan," Mary answered. She suddenly became alarmed at that point. "Hey, Joe, look over there to the right!"

"What in God's name is that?" Margaret asked. "That fenced-in area. What are all those black spots?"

"Birds..." Mary answered. "Blackbirds! It was in the paper last week. Some kind of gas came up from the ground and went up into the atmosphere and all these birds just dropped from the sky! Thousands of them! It also destroyed hundreds of acres of corn."

Margaret's eyes were bulging with amazement as Mary spoke. "It wasn't man-made, they say. It was a natural gas of some kind. Jesus said there would be plagues, Margaret."

"What else been goin' on in the world, Mary?" Joe asked while driving. "There was a huge plague in Wyoming." Mary went on.

"Hundreds of people died and they've closed the border."

Margaret sighed. "Yeah, I heard about that. It's awful. Hey, what about them computer chips?"

"We've got a little time for now." Mary answered. "Right now, it's in an experimental stage with a small population in New York State. When science gets all of the kinks worked out, I'm sure it will become law for everyone in the country to get implanted. It will replace our ID cards!"

A tear formed in Joe's eye. "My Lord, what is all this comin' to?"

Mary placed her hand on his arm. "The Lord is our Shepherd, Joe. There will be more to come. I also heard that the radical Muslim nations in the Middle East, all have nuclear weapons, plus Russia as an ally. They are warning the President to keep U.S. troops out of the Mideast, or there will be hell to pay! The President we have now may not be as sympathetic to the enemy as our last one was, but he is still in fear of the them, believe me! There's a good chance the they could take over America, Joe!"

Mary looked over at Margaret and noticed that Margaret was beginning to shake. "Look, I'm sorry, Mrs. Freeman," Mary said apologetically. "Let's just concentrate on getting to South Dakota for now. God will guide us in His will, and His peace will guard our hearts."

Tears were running down Margaret's cheeks, but yet she was faintly smiling. "Thank you, Jesus," she whispered. The RV rolled on, passing a sign that said, "Sioux City 56 Miles."

26
CHAPTER

"THIS CALLS FOR A CELEBRATION!" Rainwater announced to Tim. "I'll call the village and give them the 'all clear.'"
They finally ended up meeting in the social hall. None of them, including Tim, felt safe leaving Indian land until they were all sure that Bloomfield had really left the area. During the celebration, they also had a little meeting. They sat together in a circle, and began with a word of prayer.

"Bloomfield will be back. THAT we know!" Tim stated in a serious tone of voice. "His pride will not let him turn the other cheek. He's determined to destroy us. We need to remember the Word from the book of Ephesians. We wrestle not against flesh and blood, but against forces of darkness. Demonic forces. It's time to finish getting those caves ready! Nancy and I will have to move out of our house, as well. I've already destroyed the ID cards. Frank has offered to help out with some of those loose ends. He is not a suspect at this time so he is our only straight contact, if we have needs from the outside world. Cedar Ridge is our home now. If anyone has special needs, write them down. Frank will be stopping by tomorrow."

Rainwater then had something to add, also. "There are plenty of resources, food, and supplies here on the reservation. We put our trust in the Lord, and He always provides. You are all here for a reason, and the Lord will show us His plan. He has overcome the world!"

Stu raised his hand. "This may seem weird, but I suddenly have peace about Patty Miller. Even though she is scheduled to be executed, I believe that somehow she will have an impact on the future and the spreading of the Gospel. We should continue to pray for her deliverance."

Phil was listening intently, although at the same time, he kept leafing through his Bible. "You have a word for us, Phil, don't you?"

Phil cleared his throat. "Ah, yes in Philippians 4:8-9:"

> *"Finally brethren, whatever is true, whatever is honorable, whatever is right, whatever is pure, whatever is lovely; whatever is of good repute, if there is any excellence and if anything worthy of praise, let your mind dwell on these things. The things you have learned and received and heard and seen in me, practice these things; and the God of peace shall be with you."*

After reading this, Phil closed his Bible and began to speak. "We have much to be thankful for. Todd and I have both been hearing from the Lord on these things and it will be important to concentrate on them, and be of positive spirit—to be confident in God's ability and not our own."

Then Todd also opened HIS Bible and read Colossians 3:23-24:

> *"Whatever you do, do your work heartily, as for the Lord rather*

*than for men; knowing that from the Lord you will receive the
reward of the inheritance. It is the Lord Christ whom you serve."*
"Phil and I have been learning from Him that our work is not to be
for our own purposes, but done simply in obedience to God's will.
I sometimes want to ask why we are doing these strange things...
like the caves. We don't always have to know the reason. Just
simply act on faith. We will understand in due time." Todd was
usually the most quiet of the bunch, but when he had something
to say, it was usually profound.

As soon as they were sure that Bloomfield had left, Jennifer and
Susan went to work cleaning up a room in the back of the office and
schoolroom. A place for Tim and Nancy. Nancy would probably
need a lot of care in the near future, because it seemed that she
was slowly slipping more and more from reality, and dementia
was setting in. God would definitely have to be trusted for that
possibility.

Later that night, Tim made a list of the things he would need from
the cabin. The others made lists as well. This was going to keep
Frank very busy.

Jennifer would continue to spend time with the children. The last
time the children gathered in the schoolroom, she approached
Billy Whitebird to see if she could get him to invite his mother
to class the next morning. Jennifer felt it was time to look deeper
into Billy's situation and family life. She was especially concerned
about Billy's reluctance to talk. He relied mostly on his drawings
to be able to communicate. And they were quite alarming! Just
two days after he used the word, "Iowa," to explain his drawing of
the dead blackbirds, Jennifer heard a radio report of what indeed

had happened in Iowa, concerning the dead birds and land gas mystery. If Billy's drawings DID indeed tell of future events, Jennifer wanted to learn more about his life. The real clincher was his last picture that revealed "The Camera Man." Thanks to that revelation, the fellowship had had just enough time to find protection before Bloomfield arrived. "Is this from you, Lord?" she prayed.

Meanwhile, the RV carrying Mary and the Freemans had just left Sioux City. They had stopped there briefly to fill the gas tank and purchase some food. They chose a nice trash receptacle to toss their phones and cards into—and that was it! Now they were resisters! It would be by faith from now on.

"There's another reason I decided to take the long way," Joe said, as the RV continued down the interstate.

"What's that you say, old man?" Margaret laughed.

Joe then explained, "Yeah, well, on the way to Rapid City, about 30 miles on down the road from here, there is a homeless camp. I want to stop and see if my brother, Luther, is there. He's been missin' close to three months now!"

Margaret rubbed his shoulders to help him relax. "Then, we'll just do that!" she said. "I just don't want you to be too set on it, then get disappointed if he ain't there!"

After 30 more miles of highway, they came upon a sign identifying the camp and turned onto the access road. This particular camp was newly built and did not yet have that many residents. The largest camp was located in western Nebraska. This NEW camp was built to take the overflow, even though it was miles away. All politics and land rights, Joe figured. When they turned in, they parked in front of the chapel. Joe's brother, Luther, was a church goer, so Joe figured the chapel would be the best bet for getting information. The chaplain in charge seemed to be a loving and caring man. He informed them that he knew most of the members of his congregation by name, but he had never known anyone named Luther. Although Joe was disappointed, they stayed at the chapel and fellowshipped with the chaplain for an hour or so.

He turned out to be "old school." He was born-again. He also told them that he had no problem with the administrator of the camp when it came to teaching the Word of God. Most teaching was from memory, because he had no Bible. This stirred Mary's spirit, and she knew why they had stopped there.

"Joe, I'm goin' to run back to the RV for a sec, I'll be right back." She still had one more full Bible left—a "New American Standard, Study Edition." She returned quickly and said to the chaplain, "This is God's will that we bring this to you today."

The chaplain looked and laughed with tears. "A Bible, Lord Jesus, it's a Bible!"

"That's right," Mary said, "and it's safe. It came from a time capsule buried in the 1970s. It can't be traced."

The chaplain gently held it in his hands and leafed through it. "My prayer was answered just like that! Thank you, Jesus, and thank you folks. This is the best donation ever given to us, I promise I'll take good care of it!"

Joe then laughed. "Well, I hope you wear it out, Reverend! Wear it out, teachin' from it!"

They all embraced and the chaplain prayed for them to be protected on their journey. As they left the camp behind and returned to the highway, they were all silent for a time. Joe finally said, "Even though Luther wasn't there, God was." And he smiled through his tears.

CHAPTER

27

THE NEXT MORNING, JENNIFER'S MEETING with Billy Whitebird's mother became quite informative. Jen invited Angela to sit in, just for extra support. Billy's mom sat across from them while Billy found a small desk in the corner, where he began to draw another picture.

"Mrs. Whitebird, I asked you here hoping you can answer some questions about your son. He's a very special boy, and I'm concerned about him."

Billy's mom gave Jennifer a helpful smile. "I will say what I can," she answered.

"First I want to know about his drawings," Jennifer said. "His drawings seem to tell the future in some way. Do you know where he got this gift?"

Mrs. Whitebird sat back and relaxed. "Billy's drawings started when he visited the Spirit Cave a year ago."

Jennifer then cut in. "You mean the caves of fear?"

"No, no," Billy's mother answered. "Spirit Cave is on the other side of Tee Pee Village, a very small cave, and well hidden. Billy go there and talk with spirit and spirit teach him what to draw." Jennifer anxiously asked. "What spirit is this, Mrs. Whitebird?"

Mrs. Whitebird went on telling the story. "Billy say, spirit of Jesus. Billy not read, neither do I. Billy doesn't know Bible, but he say he knows Jesus and Jesus speak to him. Then he draws picture."

Angela looked stunned while listening in. She then joined the conversation, and asked the next question. "Does he ever try to draw pictures on his own?"

Billy's mom laughed. "He try, yes, but they are terrible, because Billy can't draw!"

Both Jennifer and Angela were perplexed. "Ok, Mrs. Whitebird, I'm also concerned about Billy not speaking more than one to three words. And he rarely even does THAT! Can you tell me why?"

"Yes," she answered.

"When Billy was younger, his father beat him. His father is okay now, but used to be addict to codeine syrup and whiskey. He lose his mind a lot. One night he hit Billy with fireplace poker! On the back of his head. We ran Billy to medical tent. Billy was unconscious many hours. When he finally wake up, he not speak for many months. Now he talk with a few words."

Just then, Billy approached them and handed a drawing to Jennifer. Angela also saw the drawing.

"My Lord!" Angela said in shock. "This is the RV that the Freemans drove when they brought me here. How could he have known?"

Jennifer then asked Billy, "What is this picture, Billy?"

He worked his mouth to form words. "They are coming here." He had said four words, which was the most he had spoken so far.

Angela then asked him, "The Freemans? They are coming back here to find me?"

Billy smiled. "With sister Mary," he said.

"Oh, Lord!" Angela stood up. "This is really for real! I can feel it around me!"

Jennifer held her composure. "So, we'll let the brothers and Susan know that we'll be getting company. We should probably get another sleeping room ready."

Angela sat back down with a look of disbelief still on her face.

Billy's mom looked concerned. "I take him home now. He get tired after drawing pictures."

"Well..." Jennifer stood and Mrs. Whitebird gave her a kiss on the cheek.

"Thank you for wanting to help my son."

"My pleasure," Jennifer answered. "With your permission, I would like to continue working with him here at school. Perhaps get his speech back and learn some reading. Would that be all right?"

"Yes," Billy's mom answered. "May the Spirit of Jesus bless you. You be Billy's teacher. Billy likes you, you will help him, please." She smiled and took Billy by the hand, and they quietly left the schoolroom together.

Jennifer then turned to Angela. "Ok, then, let's start getting ready for your friends to arrive."

THE NEXT MORNING, RAINWATER sat in his office with his usual morning coffee. Sometimes, he just had to relax and forget about the agenda, especially now, when it was starting to become overwhelming.

Just before the kids would show up for school, Jennifer usually joined him. He always looked forward to that, because he loved her company. Then, right on cue, he heard a knock at the rear door that led from the classroom. "Come on in, Jen!" he shouted, as Jennifer began to turn the door knob.

She entered the room gracefully, then plopped down on the chair in front of his desk. Rainwater stood to pour her a cup of coffee. "I'm curious about something, and so are the others, for that fact." She said.

"Ok," Rainwater responded, "and what might that be?"

"Well," she continued. "We all ditched our ID cards and cell phones, right? So why is it that you guys use cell phones at Cedar Ridge? I mean, like when you called the Tee Pee Village chief on a cell phone the day Bloomfield showed up."

Rainwater sat after the coffee was poured. "Oh, that...yes," Rainwater smiled and handed her a cup. "These are not ordinary cell phones. They're more like walkie talkies. They don't transmit through a cell tower but only from phone to phone. The range is only about two miles."

Jennifer nodded, as if satisfied. "Well, I guess that explains it, Johnnie." After a few seconds of silence, she continued. "So where are all the other guys today?"

Rainwater gave her a puzzled smile. "At the caves, is MY guess. They got a little more enthusiastic when they found out about the weather situation."

"What weather situation?" Jen asked.

"Well," Rainwater explained. "The scientists and meteorologists got together and gave a special report to the news media. Because of a huge solar flare that occurred last week, our atmosphere has been altered." He stood to pour himself another cup of coffee. "So, I guess we're not going to have much of a winter. The whole country is supposed to have summer-like weather, possible even to the middle of December, and after that, from January to March, nothing much colder than the mid 40s."

Jennifer acted surprised. "That's pretty scary, Johnny?"

Rainwater's eyebrows lifted. "Oh, well, scary, maybe, but also to our advantage—especially when you consider that most of our residents don't exactly have heat!"

Jennifer's eyes were starting to get teary, and Rainwater noticed it. "Ok," her voice quivered.

Rainwater set his coffee down. "What is going on, Jen? I mean, what is REALLY going on? Are you getting homesick?"

"Well, yeah," she said, once she was more composed. "I'm also worried about Stu's mom. She's really starting to lose it! When Stu spends time with her, she remembers who he is, but gets mixed up, and thinks he's still in high school!" Jennifer's voice started to quiver again. "She's losing her thinking capabilities fast, Johnny."

Rainwater shook his head and had a look of doubt in his eyes. "Jen! I know you well enough to see that something a lot more than that is bugging you. Now you want to try again?"

"Alright, alright," she started to cry with real tears now. "I... I can't!"

Rainwater smiled gently. "Yes, you can, Jen, you've always been able to talk to me."

Jennifer then blurted it out. "I think I'm falling in love with you!"

Rainwater's smile broadened. "If you need to be put at ease, Jen, I'm okay with that. I can respond two different ways. I can avoid you, which I don't want to do; or I could admit that I can't see my life day after day without you in it. I say the second choice is better."

Rainwater and Jennifer both stood and fell into each other's arms. When the embrace ended, Johnny said to her, "Now, since we're in love and both believers, I suppose it would be hard to continue this relationship without getting married," he paused, then spoke very tenderly. "Will you be my wife, Jennifer Houston?"

"Oh, yes!" She both laughed and cried at the same time. "Yes! Yes! Yes!"

"Ok, then," Rainwater spoke matter of factly. "I'll talk to Tim and get it arranged. Maybe Stu could be best man."

"And Susan, maid of honor," Jennifer laughed. The conversation ended just at the time they could both hear the voices of children outside the door.

"Time for school!" Rainwater announced, then they both laughed.

"Yep," Jennifer agreed. "Time for school."

WHEN THE FREEMANS FINALLY FOUND the small community outside Rapid City, where they guessed that Tim Harris lived, the Spirit led them to the Quick Lunch Diner. When they entered, they came at a time that Frank was there having lunch. After some conversation, Frank discovered they were friends of Angela, and told them they were welcome to follow his truck to Cedar Ridge. The Freemans were finally led to the dusty road that would take them to the main gate.

When they reached the gate, they were stopped by the welcoming committee. Frank went on in to Cedar Ridge, and let Angela know that she had visitors waiting outside the entrance. She ran to the gate to meet them, laughing with excitement.

"Before you drive in," she asked Joe, "did you get rid of your IDs and cell phones?"

Joe smiled. "You bet! I ditch'em in Sioux City!"

But Mary suddenly became alarmed. "Wait!" she yelled. "We forgot about license plates! Oh, no! We could have been traced!"

Fortunately, Gabe Lewis had pulled in at the same time as the Freemans. He was able to hear Mary's comments. He approached their

RV and spoke to them through the passenger window. "Nothing to worry about!" he said. "The chips in license plates only send a signal up to 500 feet. The only thing they are used for is law enforcement. When you are stopped by a cop they can do a quick scan and identify your vehicle ownership, past tickets, and so on. It helps them know if the car is stolen. That's all."

Gabe gave them a reassuring smile. The gates were finally opened, and a member of the welcoming committee waved them in.

That evening after dinner, a celebration and fellowship took place. Stories were exchanged and concerns were discussed. Mary was saddened to speak of her friends from Lincoln. She still hadn't gotten over the shock of their arrest. She knew they would most likely be sent to Scottsbluff prison, after questioning.

Rainwater and Tim managed to hook up the RV to an electrical outlet on the outside of the main building. For now, the Freemans said they would be plenty comfortable living in their vehicle. Mary found space in the schoolroom with Jennifer. Angela had been staying in the Tee Pee Village for the past few days. She loved the culture.

Stu was the only one who did not join the party that night. He wanted to spend time with his mother. He had no doubt in his mind that his remaining time with her would be short.

Jennifer and Rainwater also announced their engagement that night, which brought a round of applause and shouts of congratulations. Tim Harris had a legal license to perform marriages and in Cedar Ridge. A certificate of marriage could legally be produced. In the rapture of celebration and praise, everyone had forgotten about Bloomfield.

30
CHAPTER

THREE DAYS LATER, DURING SCHOOL TIME, Billy Whitebird drew a picture. This one took him most of the day. Jennifer could not seem to pull him away from it, even during lunch time.

At the end of the school day, he finally handed her the drawing. It was a detailed picture of Agent Bloomfield standing at Cedar Ridge's entry gate and directly behind him, an army of law enforcement men with guns. Billy was shaking and could hardly stand still. "They're coming!" Billy shouted. "Coming to kill you!"

Jennifer instantly reacted and ran into John Rainwater's offices crying and shaking. She dropped Billy's drawing on Rainwater's desk, and he slowly picked it up.

He studied it closely for a minute or two. Rainwater took it to be a valid threat! Billy had never seen Bloomfield before, yet the picture was drawn in perfect detail—it was Bloomfield, all right! He rose quickly from his chair and began pacing the floor. "Ok, Jen, we need to gather everyone we can and meet at the community center! An emergency meeting at 7:00 p.m. Got that? 7:00 p.m.! Everyone we can find."

Rainwater sat back down. "Jen? If you can make a quick run to the caves and find Tim, I'll try to get through to Angie at Tee Pee Village. Take the picture with you to show him."

Jennifer nodded her head. "Yep. 7:00 p.m. is only three hours from now. I'm on my way." She gave him a quick kiss.

"Oh," Rainwater added, "did Billy say anything else about this?" Jennifer shook her head. "Only that he was coming to kill us!"

Tim and the boys were shocked by the drawing, when they saw it, and immediately dropped the work they were doing at the time. They all piled into the panel truck and followed Jennifer back to Rainwater's office.

By the time they arrived, Rainwater had already reached Angela by phone and she was in the process of rounding up as many residents as she could find in Tee Pee village.

The first thing on Tim and Rainwater's agenda was to run down to the community center to hook up a P.A. system and set up some folding chairs. It took a bit longer than they expected, and by the time they finished, it was nearly seven o'clock. People were already beginning to show up for the meeting. When 7:00 p.m. arrived, the crowd turned out to be more than they expected. Many had to stand, because there were not enough chairs.

John Rainwater decided it was time to start, so he tested the microphone, and it squealed a couple of times. "May I get everybody's attention please? Everyone quiet down, please!" Finally, the room quieted to the sounds of only a few coughs and rustling. "I've called you here because our community is facing a very serious event! Some of you might not know that a couple weeks ago, two agents from the FBI showed up here at Cedar Ridge. They were here to apprehend innocent people! White man's law has gone insane, and they are taking away people's rights and freedom. This includes religious freedom! The FBI came with the plan to arrest some so-called fugitives that we have welcomed here as our friends!"

"I ended up having harsh words with these men, and with the help of our welcoming committee, we managed to turn them away empty-handed. But they vowed they would return and just today we received evidence that they will do just that! This time with re-enforcements! I've decided to put Cedar Ridge on alert. We may have a war on our hands if they try to force themselves upon us. When I am done speaking I would like any of those who will volunteer for guard duty combat, or strategic planning, to line up to the left of the podium. The welcome committee members will interview you and give you the details, as they see fit. Those of you out there who believe in God, and are Christians, please pray! Pray that this does not have to result in war. Most of you know the Harris family. Well, it is they, and their good friends who know and love God, that we are protecting. We are also protecting our land and our dignity! We must let the government and the FBI know that they have no place on our land, and no power under our laws. They cannot destroy us, and they cannot win in their fight against God!"

Everyone loudly applauded, and before the night's end, over 150 Native Americans volunteered for service.

Later that night, Tim joined Rainwater back in the office. "You know, John," Tim spoke quietly. "We DO want to stand for Jesus, and He taught love and compassion, not war."

Rainwater looked into Tim's eyes. "Yes," he answered. "As believers, that is true. Even towards people like Bloomfield! The other side of the coin is that I also have the responsibility as leader and protector of tribal rights. I have a duty to uphold the laws of our village."

Tim resigned himself at that point, and said to John, "In that position of leadership, you are absolutely right!"

Yet Rainwater reassured him. "Do the will of the Lord, Tim— follow Him according to your own convictions. It's good and right. As for Tribal responsibilities, I'll handle the rest, by the convictions I was given." John then added, "God's grace and direction will be with both of us, Tim." The two men shook hands, then embraced.

Stu, Jennifer, and Angela arrived a few minutes later and joined them. "So what would be the worst case scenario?" Stu asked.

Rainwater paced the floor. "Worst case scenario is that Bloomfield will consider the problem to be the entire community of Cedar Ridge staging a massive uprising against the Federal Government. He'll call in the National Guard, if necessary. If the problem escalates to the point where it spills out to surrounding communities like Rapid City, itself, the people of those communities may take sides politically and spread the chaos even further. Not to mention the lies everyone will hear through the news media. It will make Wounded Knee seem like child's play!"

Tim then gathered everyone into a circle, and they all joined hands in prayer. "Let love cast out all fear, dear God—keep us from violence and harm. Prepare our hearts to follow you, Lord. Protect the children and protect John and give him Your wisdom to make the right choices in Your will. In the name of Your Son, Jesus Christ, we ask. Amen."

SHORTLY AFTER THE ORDEAL, John Rainwater and Jennifer Houston had a small ceremony conducted by Reverend Harris. Stu stood in as best man, and Angela, as maid of honor. The Freemans donated to the cause by moving into the schoolroom for the night, so the newlyweds could have some alone time in the RV.

They were both still under stress concerning the possible visit from Bloomfield and his cronies. Because of this, they would not delay having a fellowship meeting the following morning of their short honeymoon.

During the meeting, Phil quoted what he remembered to be Patty Miller's favorite passage from Scripture. That was Colossians 3:1-4:

> *"If then you have been raised up with Christ, keep seeking the things above, where Christ is, seated at the right hand of God. Set your minds on the things above, not on the things that are on earth. For you have died and your life is hidden with Christ in God. When Christ, who is our life, is revealed, then you also will be revealed with Him in glory."*

Then also another one of her favorite verses from Galatians 2:19-20:

> *"For through the law I died to the law, that I might live to God. I have been crucified with Christ, and it is no longer I who live, but Christ lives in me; and the life which I now live in the flesh I live by faith in the Son of God, who loved me and delivered Himself up for me."*

When Phil shared these passages, the Word had a sobering effect on everyone in the room. Rainwater came to admit he was struggling with his faith since the emergency meeting at the community center. Yes, he DID have the responsibility to deal with possible threats and plan accordingly, but he was struggling with the faith it takes to trust completely in the Lord to guide his decisions. To understand that God already knew all things, understands all things and has complete power over all things.

A Scripture from the Gospel of John came to John's mind. "In the world you have tribulation, but take courage. I have overcome the world." God had the complete ability to wrap His perfect will around the situation, and bring victory!

Tim shared, by way of reminder, how Israel failed time and time again when they counted on their own power and numbers. Victory was secured when they finally surrendered all things to God, and in the days of Moses, it was not really Moses who faced the Pharoah, nor Moses who brought the plagues nor Moses who wrote the laws on tablets of stone. God did it all, and Moses was his instrument.

Now, God has written the law on human hearts, to convict the human race of sin and bring those whom He'd chosen, to the foot of the cross to believe Jesus for forgiveness and eternal life. Yes, even Bloomfield was not exempt from these truths, no matter how powerful he thought he might be.

When they all prayed together that morning, the prayer seemed to be much more centered on believing God for His will to be revealed and accomplished, rather than begging for deliverance.

Later that afternoon, the Lord received another soul into heaven. Stu had left to work in the caves that day, and his mother, Nancy, was sound asleep.

Several hours later, when Susan approached Nancy's small cot to check on her, she was under the impression that Nancy was still asleep. When Nancy could not be roused, Susan turned her over on her back and saw that her eyes were wide open and glazed over. Nancy was not breathing, and her skin was cold.

Knowing that Stu's mother had died, Rainwater jumped into his truck and drove down to the caves to break the news. The reaction was not that dramatic, because neither Tim, nor Stu, were that upset. More like relieved. They were both expecting this to happen any time, and they also knew she belonged to God through Christ.

Nancy was buried in a small canyon beneath the rocky hills. Those that attended thanked God for receiving her spirit. Many of those who attended were Native Americans from Tee Pee Village. It was now August fifth.

32

CHAPTER

At the FBI office in Omaha, on the morning of August fifth, Agent Lee Mattson joined Agent Bloomfield for a cup of coffee and some breakfast rolls.

"Did you get a chance to check into those policies?" Bloomfield asked Lee.

Lee took a sip of coffee. "Yes, I DID, Larry, and as far as I know, from what I've read in those laws, there has never been any change in policy. As far as federal law goes regarding Indian land, they are still protected with the right to rule their own roost. Unfortunately, the 'Big Chief' in charge was right about that one. These folks we are trying to pursue are under protection, and have legal asylum as long as they are in Cedar Ridge."

Bloomfield pounded the desk with his fist! "Damn it, Lee! How can we get around it?"

Lee set down his coffee and looked straight at Bloomfield. "We can grab any one of them if they step so much as one inch off that land!" he answered. "The only thing I know to do is devise a way to lure them away from Cedar Ridge somehow. Create some kind of situation that will give them a reason to chance it!"
"Like what?" Bloomfield asked.

"Well," Lee continued, "I'll give you one example. If Reverend Harris, let's say, found out that his cabin was about to be confiscated. He might risk going there to retrieve things of value. Something like that. The deal is, if we could get just one of them into custody, we would be able to negotiate with the others." "Another thing we could do," Lee went on, "is go to the front gate with a huge show of force and even though we would have to remain on our side of the gate, by law, we could demand their surrender. It might work if you could get a legal warrant from the governor of the state."

Lee paused to let that sink in, then resumed. "As a last resort, we could agitate them enough that they would get stirred up politically and stage some kind of revolt against the government. They would have to fire the first shot, so to speak. We would possibly get a green light to stop the revolt, even if we had to call in the national guard, but, Larry, it's not a good option, because it could bring a lot of bloodshed and innocent people would be killed in the crossfire!"

"Like war?" Bloomfield's eyebrows rose, as he asked that question.

"Yeah," Lee answered. "The issue would no longer be the fugitives you're after, but the entire Cedar Ridge community—if you know what I mean."

Bloomfield sat back and stretched. "I want to get something rolling no later than the 15th, so let's do some research and get a plan together—make sense?"

Bloomfield and Lee finished up their coffee and rolls, and then checked news briefings for new information about The Resistance. Lee often wondered why Bloomfield was so politically bent on enforcing the laws of The Church Act. Lawrence Bloomfield seemed to have a beyond normal zeal to send Christians to their death in Scottsbluff. It was as if he took it personally. A few weeks back, Lee he been able to ask that question of Bloomfield.

His answer was that first of all, fundamentalists generally were the type who refused to comply with the law. They would also refuse chipping, and most likely would go underground like renegades, in order to fulfill their mission. Second, they would avoid the IRS. And third, they would speak against the laws concerning gay rights, pro-choice, hate speech, and other political issues.

Christians would be against anything that disagreed with their religious viewpoints. They would use the teachings of the original Bible as an excuse for their rebellion. They would have to be sent to the wall, just like Patty Miller, because their roots are planted too deeply for any hope of rehabilitation!

Bloomfield also had personal reasons for his rage. In his childhood upbringing, his father and mother were both strict conservative Baptists. Lawrence was forced to read the Bible, attend Sunday School and Youth Group, not allowed to have normal friendships, or attend High School prom. He was laughed at and bullied by his peers in school, and written off as an "oddball." Bloomfield could hardly wait to turn 18 and flee. Once he got clear of his parents, he studied law and joined the FBI. Now, at this present time, he jumped at the chance for vengeance, and since The Church Act came into play, it made much of that vengeance—legal.

ON THE MORNING OF THE SEVENTH, back at Cedar Ridge, Susan and Mary decided to pay a visit to the Freemans. Since they had arrived, the Freemans had spent a lot of time closed off from the others. Joe and Margaret seemed to be isolating themselves and hiding behind the closed door of their RV, although the Freemans opened their door freely after Susan knocked. "We were concerned about you two isolating yourselves, to be honest!" Susan said as they all settled around the RV's small, pull-out table.

Joe scratched his head. "I admit, I'm not comfortable around folks when I'm scared or confused. I'm afraid I'll act strange around them." Margaret nodded her head in agreement.

Margaret spoke shyly. "I feel that way, too. I don't know what to make of all this. I feel trapped sometimes. Don't get me wrong now, I'm thankful for God's miracles and I know we are safer here than any place else, but I also realize it is not safe to ever leave. I'm just not used to these changes."

"I know it's hard sometimes," Mary comforted. "God used you both to rescue me from that fruit cellar—I'll always be grateful that you listened to God and found me."

Joe placed his hand on Mary's arm and gave it a gentle squeeze. He shook his head. "It's like ol' Satan set a huge trap. He's got it all worked out on how to put God's children in bondage."

Susan asked Joe for his Bible. "I got a verse to share, Joe." He handed her the Bible and she opened it to the Hebrews 12. She then looked up and said to them, "Remember in Hebrews 11, where the Word gives an account of all those believers who were persecuted over the years? The one thing that kept them going was that they knew about those things which cannot be seen in THIS world. Like a city made without hands, built by God in the heavens. Well, they were to be examples to us and one thing we learn from them is that they were not all given a way out physically, but were given the grace to endure, even to the point of death."

As they listened to Susan, Joe put his arm around his wife, and drew her close to him. Susan had their full attention at this point.

Susan looked down at the Bible in her lap and began to read from Hebrews 12:

> *"Therefore since we have so great a cloud of witnesses surrounding us, let us also lay aside every encumbrance, and sin which so easily entangles us, and let us run with endurance the race that is set before us, fixing our eyes on Jesus, the author and perfecter of faith, who for the joy set before Him endured the cross, despising the shame, and has sat down at the right hand of the throne of God. For consider Him who has endured such hostility by sinners against Himself, so that you may not grow weary and lose heart."*

She then closed the Bible and looked up at them. "Just think—if we could only just see by faith the promises and rewards when He returns for us, and see them more clearly than we see our hassles on earth. I know we don't possess this power on our own. But with the Lord giving us His grace and peace, we can be able to see HIS plan more clearly than the WORLD'S plan."

Mary then agreed with Susan. "We can't leave Indian land, that's true, but there is much to do right here on the reservation."

"You're both right," Joe admitted. "The Word you gave is for real. We'll pray for more guidance. Hey, pretty lady," he turned toward Margaret. "What do you say about joining the others for lunch today? That will be a big step!"

Susan and Mary both knew their trip to see the Freemans was not wasted. They all ended up praying together and confessing their sins of anxiety and doubt. The Holy Spirit filled them, and they were returned to fellowship.

All the believers at Cedar Ridge would find out that even though the will of God was simple, it was not always easy.

Now, Frank from the hardware store was also joining in more and more as he helped Tim and the boys prepare the caves. They had made quite a bit of progress over the past week. The caves were well stocked with food, blankets, and lanterns. They found passages and tunnels within that had comfy spots to sit or sleep, without hardly any draft from the front entrances.

What puzzled Tim and Stu the most was that they still did not clearly know the reason for all these preparations. They knew they were already relatively safe on Indian land, but the Lord knew all things. The things of the future. For the time being, it was a mystery in human understanding. Nevertheless, they figured by the end of the day the preparations would be adequate enough to begin concentrating on other things: things such as, how to handle Bloomfield.

Tim had doubts about that issue. Was there an exception in the federal laws, regarding Cedar Ridge? Something perhaps written between the lines? An exception to the rule that would somehow give the FBI jurisdiction and access? The fugitives that Bloomfield sought personally were not true Native Americans, and mostly not residents of South Dakota at all. Would that change things legally? Tim left the cave and picked up a rock to throw. "What am I thinking?" he said out loud to himself.

"Yes?" he heard Phil's voice right behind him, and it made him jump.

Tim turned toward Phil, "Oh, I just said 'what am I thinking?' I've been reasoning with myself again, and forgetting that we are under God's protection, not just Rainwater's. Not only that, but whatever happens—capture, EMP, nuclear war—we are STILL under His care and grace."

"I know what you mean, Mr. Harris." Phil commented.

"Yes," Tim continued, "Doggone it! I find it so hard sometimes, to keep my eyes on the Lord and remember that His power, His love, and His plan far exceeds worldly law, Bloomfield, or whatever else comes along. I'm concerned about Frank, though. He is still living in his store on government land. So far, Bloomfield has never mentioned his name, so I have no clue whether Frank has been connected with us. Frank may have already been spotted with us by some crazy federal agent up in the hills with a telescope, for all I know."

Phil then said to Tim, "If you're concerned, Mr. Harris, maybe you should talk to him. This might be a warning in your spirit from God." "Yep," Tim then agreed. "I'll talk to him about it. I don't think that Frank wants to end up as bait in the enemy's hands. He sure doesn't want to leave his precious hardware store, I know. I was thinking maybe we could find more room in one of the buildings around here, where he could store all his merchandise. Since we can't leave here to help him move all that stuff, it poses a problem." Well," Phil responded, "God will have to speak to his heart."

Phil, Stu, and Todd climbed into Tim's truck and they left the caves behind for the day. Frank had said earlier that he would be joining them for dinner at the schoolhouse. Tim would talk to him then.

34

CHAPTER

Angela and Jennifer spent the day of the seventh at the school room. The children were going forward one-by-one, to the blackboard. Then Jennifer would write a word on the board for each child to read and to speak. Billy Whitebird did not participate. He was withdrawn and silent.

He had not drawn any pictures for a week, but on this day, he finally got up from his desk, and approached the blackboard, when the other children were finished. He picked up a stubby piece of chalk and drew a cross on the board. He then pointed to it, and said, "Trust!" Both Angela and Jennifer rejoiced. They were immediately filled with peace.

When God spoke through Billy, they began to notice the power of the Holy Spirit. Jennifer remembered the words of Paul the Apostle. "And my message and my preaching were not in persuasive words of wisdom, but in demonstration of Spirit and of power, that your faith should not rest on the wisdom of man, but on the power of God."

She spoke these words out loud to Angela, who smiled and said, "oh, yes, Jen—1 Corinthians 2. The first five verses, give or take." They were both filled with joy and the power of God at that moment.

Then Angela quoted from that same chapter. "For I determined to know nothing among you except Christ and Him crucified."

Billy Whitebird returned to his desk, but continued to point at the blackboard saying, "Trust! Trust!"

Frank showed up for supper that night, just as he said he would. Also the Freemans joined them, which was a joyful surprise to everyone. After a good meal of fried chicken and scalloped potatoes, Tim got his opportunity to talk with Frank privately.

Tim encouraged him to go with him on a little stroll around the grounds, so they could converse.

"So, what's on your mind, Tim? You look a little uptight!"

Tim looked at the ground. "I think it's time for you to move to Cedar Ridge, Frank."

Frank brushed back his thin hair. "Why so soon? I got a store to run."

Tim had expected that kind of a response from Frank. "Look, Frank, I've got a serious feeling in my gut, and in my spirit, for that matter." Tim looked at the ground again. "You know it didn't take long for Bloomfield to connect the dots on Gabe Lewis. They had him in custody, as you know. It was only by the grace of God that he wasn't forced to leave with Bloomfield and end up in Scottsbluff prison. Thank God he was able to stay here with us!"

Frank smiled faintly, but his lips twitched. "I don't know how to do it! Look, Tim, I thought about moving my merchandise from the store, and relocate here where I can be of good use. It's hard to just walk away. I spent 12 years getting that store off the ground."

Tim looked Frank in the eye. "Frank, the Bible teaches us. In the words of Jesus, 'He who loves his life in this world, will lose it, but he who loses his life for MY sake, will find it.' You have to make a decision like that in your own heart by faith. Look at Gabe! After Bloomfield left him here, he wasn't even able to leave here long enough to get a change of clothes, or say goodbye to his friends in the department! Look at him now, Frank! He's never had joy and fulfillment like this, his whole life. He thanks God every day for saving him from execution. I don't want to see YOU in cuffs, Frank, and believe you me, Bloomfield WILL find out you've been helping us, if he doesn't know already!"

Frank shook his head. "Man, what could be worse?"

Tim continued. "What could be worse is that he could use you for bait to try to make the rest of us surrender, and we would, in order to save your life. In the end, it wouldn't. He'd probably kill us all anyway."

Frank had a guilty look. "So, what do you propose, Tim?"

"I propose we start right now!" he answered, "you don't return to the store at all. I'll find a room and a bunk for you. Don't even leave to get anything."

Frank jumped nervously at that. "Now, that is sudden! If I stay right now, then what can be done about the items in the store that we will ALL need?"

Tim smiled. "I prayed about it earlier, Frank. It's simple. We can send a couple of Indian brothers from here to gather a list of stuff from the store. Bloomfield isn't interested in arresting any Native Americans. Just give them your shop key and we'll send them into town. You can give them a signed note saying that they have permission to run things at the store, while you are on vacation. Simple enough?"

God then spoke to Frank's heart and opened his eye. "The Spirit is speaking to me, Tim. Wow! God wants me to trust Him by faith, like you said. He's showing me not to gather treasures on earth, but treasures in heaven." Frank stopped pacing and stood rock solid before Tim. "I don't understand it all just yet," he smiled, "but I'm staying! Yes, I'll stay!"

Tim gave him a brotherly slap on the back—and they both laughed with joy.

Tim and Frank walked back to the school together and the whole fellowship rejoiced over Frank's decision. Rainwater told Frank that he had already found a couple of volunteers to take care of the store.

"Do you have any family, Frank?" Rainwater asked. "If so, we could probably get word to them about your location here."

Frank turned sad. "My wife died six years ago. I DO have a 22-year-old son named Jason, but he's way up north in Rugby, North Dakota. The sad part is that he doesn't have the Lord in his life, not yet, anyway." Frank was no longer smiling. "He goes to one of the Universal Churches up there. He believes all that poison from the Common Bible!" Everybody gathered around Frank when he said that, and they all began to pray for Jason. Frank cried for the first time in 6 years. That "tough guy" face of his was broken in pieces by God's love. "Thank you, Folks!" he sobbed. "I can't thank you enough." Now was the time for celebration to honor Cedar Ridge's newest resident.

BLOOMFIELD AND AGENT MATTSON were once again having their morning ritual together of coffee and breakfast rolls. It was the morning of the eighth.

"Ok, Lee," Bloomfield wiped his mouth with a napkin. "So you say we got three options? Lure them out; convince them we have authority to demand the fugitives be released to us; or provoke them to violence, right?"

"Right!" Lee answered.

Then Bloomfield paced the floor as he went on. "No way I can go with the provoke idea just yet. I wouldn't want to attempt a battle against civic violence without plenty of manpower in advance. That kind of support is not easy to get right now! I guess we'll have to start at square one, and try to lure them out. Any ideas?"

"Maybe one," Lee answered.

"When we were taking that idiot Sheriff to the gate we were allowed in mostly because we had their beloved Sheriff in custody, remember?"

Bloomfield cut in. "So, what's your point, Lee?"

"Well, Lawrence, we need to find another guy like the Sheriff, who we know is helping them. We bust him or her, and we use it as a bargaining chip. They either surrender, or we send their friend to the wall! Or we threaten to shoot 'em on the spot!"

Lee took another sip of coffee. "To start with, I think we should pack and go back to Rapid City. We can follow up from there. Maybe make an appointment with the governor, while we're at it. We may even discover new options we haven't thought of yet. I also think we oughta' check out that storekeeper at the hardware store. When we were on our way up the main road that leads to the gate, I saw a truck coming from the opposite direction. A truck that was leaving Cedar Ridge. I'm pretty sure that the guy drivin' it was him."

"Ok, Lee, "I guess that's a start! I'll go online and get some plane tickets to South Dakota. Start gettin' your stuff together!"

It seemed that Tim Harris was correct in his spiritual discernment. He indeed had heard from God regarding Frank. Bloomfield and Lee connected some more dots, *but not in time.* The believers at Cedar Ridge, under the Lord's leading, were always one step ahead.

Two men from the welcoming committee were also sent out that day to check on the store. They drove Rainwater's truck in order to do some hauling. The list of items they carried was made up of mostly survival items—lanterns, kerosene, binoculars, boots for climbing, canteens, a tent, and surprisingly, more guns. Frank's store had a rack of 30 or so—mostly hunting rifles. Of course, they would also need plenty of ammo. The two men were slightly nervous about the guns. Was Rainwater really expecting a war? They hoped not, yet they knew he was serious when he made that speech at the community center. Rainwater seemed to have no doubt that Cedar Ridge was in danger of a siege. He had sent a memo that morning announcing another community meeting to be held at 7:00 p.m. Rainwater was not one to request a meeting, unless it was serious. All would attend, of course.

That morning, Rainwater had a flash! I guess you could call it "a stroke of wisdom." He shared it with Jennifer and they both agreed to send the memo for a meeting. Johnny and Tim had a long conversation that same morning. Rainwater had to make it clear to the entire village that no matter how the enemy might try to provoke them, they were not to return threats. And nobody from Cedar Ridge was to EVER fire the first shot—they were to remain silent. The FBI had no authorization to even enter the front gate, unless they had lawful reasons that we okayed by the governor of South Dakota. If the Indians posed any threat to the outside community, *that* could give the governor cause to make such an agreement!

At 7:00 p.m. that night, Rainwater was very clear on this agenda. Everyone raised their hands in understanding and agreement. They all agreed to take caution in dealing with the enemy, and to give Bloomfield no legal excuse to attack Cedar Ridge.

ONE MINOR DRAWBACK for those living a new life at Cedar Ridge was the tendency to be so focused on that life that they began to withdraw from some interests in the events of the outside world. A lot of fundamental Christians have had that impression on people for years. Just like the old saying, "You're so heavenly minded that you're no earthly good." It was true from teachings in the Word, of course, that believers were to derive their peace and strength from the Lord.

Believers needed to walk by faith and in understanding of those things unseen from God's Word, rather than by the evening news. Yet, the other side of the coin was that a spiritual walk in God's power was necessary in order to be prepared and respond to the situations they would face in the world in which they live. They need to also not rule out God's leading in preparation.

Tim understood these things perhaps, more than the others. He didn't rule out the idea of the caves being for the purpose of sheltering God's chosen during a massive attack against the United States. Tim had a concern about the world outside of Cedar Ridge, and knew that living in Cedar Ridge did not make the rest of the world disappear.

There were events going on daily. Massive earthquakes on the western seaboard, economic collapse, and threats of nuclear war. There were also millions of men and women in homeless camps, and Christians being put to death in Scottsbluff, all because the world had gone mad. Many believers over the years had derived comfort in believing Christ would return or the Rapture would occur before the bad stuff really hit the fan. Many never realized the possibility that prophecy was well-balanced with the events of the Middle East, like in the rise of Islam, the appearance of the Antichrist, and Armageddon. Even then, God never promised to exempt believers from hardship before these fulfillments. The Word of God also described the Last Days as a time when people's love would grow cold and the church would fall away from the faith. Persecution had been rampant since the first century. In modern society, many believers were under the impression that because they lived in America, they had freedom.

Even those members of the Government-run universal church with its Common Bible, believed they lived in the Christian nation. It was hard for those who grew up in free America to see the bigger picture. That the whole world lies in wickedness and the only hope is eternal life in Christ Jesus.

It was an amazing deception to believe that America was a free Christian nation. It was America that removed God from public schools; corrupted the marriage bed; removed God's true Word from their pulpits; ran away when Israel needed an ally; condemned those who believe God's true Word to be guilty of hate speech.

From time-to-time, the believers at Cedar Ridge still prayed for Patty Miller, because she was one of their own, yet most of them were inwardly still afraid to know what was really going on in the world as a whole, including Rainwater and Tim. Cedar Ridge had no cable or satellite TV, no newspapers, and hardly any communication with the outside. Tim decided it was time to change some of that!

Now, in the community center, was a DVD player and a radio. When the two men were sent out to check on Frank's store and pick up supplies, Tim gave them another list as well. DVD's that deal with news and world events, newspapers, and news magazines—and also a stop in at Quick Lunch, to listen to the latest gossip.

Tim had the wisdom to know that even though his sustenance and very existence depended on who he was "in Christ," he also knew about all those Scriptures that warned believers to "watch, therefore" or what Paul the Apostle said regarding Satan, "We are not ignorant of his schemes." He knew that Jesus warned that if a man did not know how to interpret simple things such as the coming of rain, how could he discern the signs of the times? Also, when the disciples showed interest in the coming events of the future, Jesus did not hesitate to share it with them what was written in Matthew 24. The events surrounding the world we live in must have had some importance, otherwise, Jesus Himself would not have bothered to dedicate any time to it.

The believers at Cedar Ridge now had a name. That name in worldly circles was "The Resistance." The conviction in Tim's heart on this day, the ninth of August, was not so much to focus on all the depressing tragedy of the world, but rather to teach and learn a spiritual way of life by faith; to exist in it, and challenge it in the will of God.

Tim knew that the glorious life they could all know in Christ was, in fact, true! Yet, he also knew that those who bury their heads in the sand can become a danger to themselves and the others that they love.

Patty Miller was a prime example. Would it have been that hard just to stay off the internet? By acting indiscreetly, many lives were endangered. Yet, Patty's zeal was still respected, and knowing that God causes all things to work together for the good to those who love Him, they felt they had no right to question the overall purpose.

37
CHAPTER

The following day, the tenth of August, both men from the welcoming committee returned from town center early in the afternoon. One of them handed Tim a shopping bag. "This is for YOU, Reverend," he said.

When Tim emptied the bag on his cot, he found some items of interest. 2 DVD's—one was titled *Top News Stories of the 21st Century;* the other was titled, *When Freedom Dies! The End of Free Speech in America!* Tim also found several back issues of *Time Magazine* and *USA Today.* Tim figured that after sorting through all the propaganda, these goodies were reputable enough to at least get most of the facts. Tim's heart sank every time he thought about the situation they all faced in their own little world at Cedar Ridge.

The enemy was coming! Tim *knew* that. He also knew The Resistance was now being made ready, and not only in Cedar Ridge. There would be others.

DAY OF RESISTANCE

PART THREE: BLOODSHED

BLOOMFIELD LOOKED ONLINE in an attempt to book a flight to Rapid City. He discovered there were no longer any direct flights. The only space he could find was a flight to San Francisco that had a stop in Rapid City, but only after first flying to Des Moines, Iowa. After a two-hour delay in Iowa, it went to Rapid City. To top it off, the only space available on that flight was one seat the morning of the 10th, and one seat on the morning of the 11th. Bloomfield quickly booked both flights. He would send Agent Lee out on the 10th, then join him the next day. Inconvenient, yes, but it would get the job done.

Lee came close to missing his flight, but boarded just in time before the gate door was closed. After two boring hours at the Des Moines airport, he finally arrived in Rapid City, and drove a rental car to the small community near Cedar Ridge. This time he found nice lodging at a place called Rocky Point Lodge. When he checked in, he dumped his baggage, then returned to the town center to do some snooping.

It did not take him long to discover that Frank from the hardware store was supposedly on vacation. Lee doubted that. Frank was most likely in hiding, to Lee's way of thinking. He decided to stop in next door at the Quick Lunch Café to see if he could locate the waitress he had met on his last visit. She might have some information, yet

Lee was suspicious of her association with Reverend Harris. She was probably protecting the fugitives.

He entered the café with the sound of the juke box blasting "Summertime Blues" by Eddie Cochran. The waitress he had met was not in the café at the time, but he found out from the manager that her name was Lilly—Lilly Munson. The café manager gave Lee directions to the ranch house that Lilly shared with her father. When Lee finally found the place, a man was outside in the front of the house changing a tire on his truck. Lee assumed he must be Lilly's father. Lee approached him. "Sir?"

"Yeah, who are you?" the man answered, sounding irritated.

"Agent Lee Mattson, FBI!" Lee loved saying that to people—it made him feel important and powerful. The man stood up after tightening one of the lug nuts on the tire, still holding the tire iron in his left hand.

"Howard Munson." He wiped his right hand on his jeans and finally shook hands quickly with Lee. "What does the FBI want with me?" he asked, with a tone of hostility.

Lee answered, "It's not YOU I have come to see. I'm looking for your daughter, Lilly."

"Lilly, oh, yes," Mr. Munson responded. "She went fishing with her boyfriend. Won't be back fer' a couple hours. What you want her for?" He was beginning to act more agitated.

"To question her, Mr. Munson. About her involvement with Reverend Timothy Harris and his friends from Omaha."

Mr. Munson returned to his lug nuts. "She's got nothin' to do with that! Are they guilty of a crime, or somethin'?"

"Yes, Mr. Munson, I'm afraid so! Also, I believe your daughter may have played a part in helping them to avoid arrest!"

"Ah, yes," Munson shouted. "I remember seein' it in the paper. You fellas arrested Sheriff Lewis and had a scuffle with them Indian folks up on Cedar Ridge, right?"

"That was us, I guess," Lee answered, a bit defensively.

Mr. Munson stood again and shouted at Lee. "Well, then, you better jus' get your skinny ass back in your car, and get the hell off my land then!"

"Oh, really?" Lee's eyebrows raised. "No, instead, I think I'll just keep you company until your daughter gets back. How does THAT sound, Pard'ner?"

Mr. Munson went back to his lug nuts again. "Whatever you say, Mr. FBI! Just stay out of my way while I get these tires changed."

Lee turned his back on Munson and looked about, admiring the beauty of the land. He decided to try and make nice with Munson. "You've got such a nice…"

Lee never finished the sentence. He was abruptly silenced by Munson's tire iron smashing into the back of his skull. Lee most likely was dead before he hit the ground. He was hit so hard that the back of his skull caved into his brain.

Mr. Munson panicked at first, but then quickly composed himself. He needed to get rid of the body! He had to act quickly, because he wanted to be home when Lilly returned. He finished tightening the lug nuts as fast as possible, and loaded Lee's body in the passenger side of the truck. He drove into Indian territory to try and find a desolate spot. Munson spotted the area right below the three caves, and pushed the body out onto the rocks. "No time to get the body out of sight," he thought, but then really didn't worry about it. The Indians would be the suspects, not him.

He drove back home and was relieved that Lilly was still gone. He began guzzling beer from the fridge to try and calm down. He hoped there was still time to get the truck cleaned up, before Lilly got home. He tried his best, but left a few stains near the door handle. He cleaned all of the trash and empty beer cans out of the seats, and replaced the floor mats.

When he finally returned to the house, he guzzled some more beer. He knew he needed to play a role, and a darn good one. Being a little bit drunk was not unusual to his daughter; however, he was still worried about the fact that his daughter seemed to have finely tuned radar concerning her father. She always noticed if his behavior was odd. Howard Munson kept repeating to himself as he drank his beer. "What have I done?" He justified his guilt by believing he was protecting his little girl, like any father would. The thought of her being arrested, charged, and sent to Scottsbluff was unacceptable. Agent Lee was dead! Munson had killed him! "Time would pass." He thought. "The Indians would be blamed." All he had to do was wait it out, until people forgot about the dead FBI agent.

EARLY ON THE MORNING OF THE 11TH, Tim, Stu, Phil, and Todd jumped into the truck and drove to the caves. They went just to check things over, and make sure nothing was left undone.

When Tim's truck pulled up to the base of the cliff, he slammed on his brakes! Everyone sitting in the back toppled forward.

Phil jumped out of the truck bed, followed by the others. "What's going on, Mr. Harris?"

Just as Phil was asking this question, Tim shouted, "Look!" He pointed off to the side of the road, where the crumpled body of a man lay among the rocks.

They slowly approached and saw that he was not moving. He was laying facedown where the back of his caved-in skull was plainly visible. "My Lord, this guy either fell from the cliff and bashed his head on the rocks, or he was murdered and left here." Tim leaned over the body as he spoke.

Stu then asked Tim, "Can you identify him?" Tim turned the body over to see the man's face, and gasped. The boys did not recognize him, but Tim did.

"You guys would not have seen this man the day he came here with Bloomfield. You were all at the Tee Pee Village. He's an FBI agent that came with Bloomfield that day. Agent Lee was his name, if I recall correctly."

"So, what do you think happened, dad?" Stu asked. Stu felt nauseated, and his voice quivered a bit.

"He might have known about the caves," Tim answered, "although I kind of doubt it, because, even if he knew, how would he have known these caves were the right ones, with so many of them in the area? And if the caves had NO significance, what would he be doing wandering around out here by himself?" Tim scratched his gray beard and continued. "I think he was murdered, and then dumped here! What I don't understand is why he was dumped out in the open like this, when he could have been dumped in the canyon, where he wouldn't be found! Unless he was left here so that he WOULD be found...and when they found his body here on Indian land, we would be the suspects, or perhaps Rainwater and his welcoming committee."

Stu gave Tim a confused look. "Do you think maybe someone from the reservation might have really done this, Dad?"

"No, Stu," Tim answered. "Why would they? He had no jurisdiction on this land anyway. And everyone knew that."

Phil then spoke up. "I think someone from the town center did it, and wanted the blame to fall on us!"

"Well, we got a real problem now!" Stu chimed in. "Bloomfield is probably around somewhere looking for his friend, so we need to decide what to do."

"We'll do the honest thing and report it, is what we'll do!" Tim stated. Everyone felt a chill, yet they all knew that in the eyes of the Lord, they must do the right thing. After thinking things over for a while, Tim finally spoke. "C'mon, let's get in the truck and drive back to the village. We'll have to send one of the others to town. Obviously, we can't leave Cedar Ridge ourselves, so we'll send a couple guys. If Bloomfield wants to talk to me personally, we'll have to meet at the gate and talk through the fence. This is the Devil's work, brothers, and this time he cooked up a real dilly!"

When they returned to the reservation, they went straight to Rainwater's office and told him the whole story. Rainwater deliberated for quite a while. He was stunned, and confused about what to do. Finally, he took Tim's advice and sent two men from the welcoming committee into town. The first thing they did when arriving in town, was to let themselves into Frank's store to use his phone. They called the Rapid City Police to report the incident, and told the police that the body that had been found was Agent Lee Mattson from the FBI.

One hour later, Lawrence Bloomfield landed at Rapid City's airport, not yet knowing the news of his friend's murder.

Bloomfield had been concerned, because Agent Mattson had agreed to be at the lodge when Bloomfield arrived. Bloomfield called from the airport more than once, but Lee didn't answer his cell phone. Bloomfield thought maybe his cell phone battery was either dead, or Lee's cell couldn't get a signal from that location. Nevertheless, he was disturbed about it.

When Bloomfield entered the terminal to pick up his luggage, he heard an announcement over the intercom. "Lawrence Bloomfield, please report to the courtesy desk. Lawrence Bloomfield, please report. This is an emergency!"

Once he located the courtesy desk, he found himself in the presence of the Rapid City police. "We didn't know where to find you," the office explained. "We found on the airline register that you were on this flight. I'm afraid we have bad news, Sir."

"Well," Bloomfield barked, "quit talking in circles and come out with it, man!"

"One of your agents, Lee Mattson, was found dead, Sir. Near the Cedar Ridge reservation. We suspect it was murder."

Bloomfield was devastated! He grabbed the officer by the arm to steady himself. Lee had been his best friend.

THAT NEXT AFTERNOON, Bloomfield parked his rented Jeep Cherokee about 50 yards from the fence at Cedar Ridge. As usual, the welcoming committee was there to greet him. "Hey! Get Big Chief and the Reverend on the line! Tell them to get their butts out here NOW!"

One of the Indians responded to Bloomfield's request. "We don't appreciate disrespect! Try asking."

"Ok, can you please do that for me?" Bloomfield's tone was NOT friendly—he was mocking them.

The same Indian radioed Rainwater's office. "That guy from the FBI is here. He wants to see you and the Reverend, and he doesn't look friendly."

About 10 minutes later, Tim and Rainwater came strolling slowly toward the fence. Bloomfield waited until they were close enough to not have to shout. "I talked to the State Governor today, fellas. In about 24 hours or so, I will have authorization to investigate about the murder of my agent! And you WILL allow me in to question people, as I see fit! Got that, Chief?"

Rainwater answered, but not in friendly fashion. "You will not take on step on this land, Bloomfield!"

"If I have a signed letter from the Governor, I will!" he shouted back. Then he calmed a bit. "Look, is that any way to talk to me, Chief? Why do you want to prevent an investigation? It's my job. I need to know who killed my friend."

Rainwater also calmed himself. "It was no one who lives here. That is, if it was really murder to begin with. We had a meeting with all the residents, Sir, we all agreed not to cause any trouble with the FBI."

Bloomfield ruffled up a bit. "So, just because YOU tell me that your people have a code of conduct, that makes it so? No one EVER breaks the rules?"

Tim then spoke. "This could be a fruitful conversation, if it wasn't for the fact that it won't end with the investigation of Agent Lee's death! You intend to go the extra mile and try to arrest our Christian friends, and see that they are sent to the wall! True or not?"

Bloomfield was silent, and his silence gave him away.

"Like I said," Rainwater cut in, "you won't set foot on this land!"

Bloomfield's face reddened. "With legal procedure through the Governor's office, I will!" He shouted like a spoiled child, whose candy was taken away. "Besides, what will you do to stop me? Shoot me?"

Rainwater was getting fed up with this childish dialogue. "If we believe you came here to violate the rights of our people and do harm to us, yes, we'll shoot you, if you try to enter our village by force!" Then in a calmer voice, Rainwater added, "You might be welcome to investigate if you can agree that it is ALL you do."

Bloomfield couldn't respond to that. His motives were more about cuffing Christians, than they were about investigating Lee's death, although he would do *that*, as well.

Bloomfield finally turned to walk away, but turned back toward Rainwater before he reached his Jeep. "I'll be back with a letter from the Governor, Big Chief!"

"And you will still not set foot on this land!" Rainwater shouted back. Bloomfield returned to his vehicle and peeled out, leaving a cloud of dust.

"Did you really mean that?" Tim asked Rainwater later, in the privacy of the office.

"Damn straight, Tim!" he answered. "If he comes back with the intentions of harming innocent people, one of which is my wife, I have the responsibility to protect them—Governor or not!"

Rainwater sadly shook his head and brushed the hair out of his eyes. "According to the messed up laws in Bloomfield's world, a man is guilty for learning and teaching the Truth. But by God's law in His Word, Bloomfield is the guilty one! God taught me, Tim, that even if the whole world lives in a lie, let God be true. I must do what is right."

Tim thought to himself that if only his life was at stake, he would surrender for the sake of Cedar Ridge, but it wasn't that simple. He had to consider the others, as well. He knew Bloomfield would not leave without getting ALL of them! This included Sheriff Lewis and the Freemans, also.

"How can a man *hate* so much?" he finally asked Rainwater.

"It's not just HIM," he answered. "Our battle is not against flesh and blood, remember? We are talking about the Devil, Tim! America has all gone wrong! The Devil hates everything about God's plan—we must remember that! It's not just Bloomfield."

LILLY MUNSON ARRIVED TO WORK a bit early on the morning of the 12th. Quick Lunch usually did not have many customers until 11:00 a.m. Although they served breakfast, more patrons arrived during the lunch hour. Lilly decided to sit and relax with a hot cup of coffee, before starting her shift.

As she sat at a booth near the window, the manager approached. "May I sit, Lilly?"

Lilly smiled. "Of course, Martha, please do."

Her boss looked a bit distraught. "Lilly, when you were gone the last couple days, that news guy came in asking for you."

Lilly sat up, alarmed! "He's not a news guy, he's FBI! What did you tell him?"

"Well," looking ashamed, her boss replied, "I told him where to find you."

"Martha! You told him where I lived? Luckily, I was out fishing my first day off—I got home late last night, but I guess he never stopped in anyway."

"Lilly!" Martha looked shocked. "He never stopped in, because he's dead!"

"Wait a minute!" Lilly raised her hands in the air.

"Yes, Lilly, it's true. They found him up in the hills near the caves. They think it was murder!"

Lilly said nothing for a long time, but thoughts were going through her head. "It couldn't be," she thought. "If he stopped by on the 10th, my dad would have been home that day." Her dad had never mentioned anyone stopping by.

"It's in the *Rapid City Extra*. Right here!" Martha said, as she plopped the newspaper on the table in front of Lilly.

Lilly glanced through the article. Agent Lee was found on the morning of the 11th, which meant he was probably killed on the 10th.

"Martha?" she said in a weak, shaky voice. "Can I use one more of my sick days? I don't feel so good."

Martha thought a minute. "Sure, Kid, go home. I've got Ivy coming in today, and I doubt I'll really need you—sure, go!"

Lilly raced for her white Nissan, and drove toward home as fast as she could go. When she arrived, it appeared that her father had already left for work, but he didn't take the truck. Sometimes one of his friends picked him up for work in the morning.

Lilly slowly walked over to the truck. The first thing she noticed was the tire iron lying on the ground, next to the driver's side. When she picked it up, she examined it closely, and saw a small splatter of reddish colored goo of some kind. She then looked inside the truck to see what else she could find. The front seat of the truck was cleaned out of all the trash. The seat covers had been cleaned and the floor mats, replaced. This was out of character for her dad. He never gave a rip what the truck looked like inside. Then she noticed it! Right near the passenger side door handle— another small spot of that reddish brown goo. She was afraid of her father sometimes, because he had a violent temper, especially when he drank.

She ran back to her car and drove to the nearest gas station, to pick up a copy of the *Rapid City Extra*, in order to read more of the article. She read as she sat in her car. She found out that the body was dumped on Indian land near the cliff caves, about a quarter mile south of the main gate to Cedar Ridge.

Then, she was astonished to read that it was obvious he was beaten to death with a heavy, blunt object; something probably steel or iron. She drove back to the house and once again walked over to her father's truck and looked all around the ground surrounding it. Right near the fence, about six feet away, she saw splotches on the ground. She looked closer—more goo!

"Blood," she said out loud. "Blood!" She ran into the house and sat in her bedroom with the door locked. "I can't tell anyone,"she thought. "I'll go back to work tomorrow and act normal." She hoped by then she would be calm enough that no one would notice anything wrong, but her fear got the best of her, and she ran back to her car, and left the property. She would find a place to go for awhile. She didn't want to be home when her father got back! She left a note by the fridge, "I'll be home late. Don't wait up. There are leftovers in the fridge. Lil."

The thought *did* occur to her that the people of Cedar Ridge might be accused of this tragedy. She would wait awhile, and see. Maybe the case would never be solved. She bombed down the highway, until she spotted the Econolodge by the road side. She checked in for the night, and called her boyfriend.

42

CHAPTER

LATE IN THE AFTERNOON OF THE 12TH, Bloomfield was back in Rapid City, seated in the governor's office. Governor Richardson looked and acted put out, and exasperated.

"Bloomfield! I told you I would not have your authorized document ready until tomorrow. What are you doing here?"

"There was a slight complication," Bloomfield answered. He cleared his throat. "I had a chat with the Big Chief earlier today. He threatened to shoot me, if I entered Cedar Ridge, without a letter from you."

"Well, *that's interesting*," the governor responded. "First of all, his name is not Big Chief, it's John Rainwater, and he is a highly educated man. Educated enough to never make a statement like that, unless there were reasons besides your murder investigation."

"There is, Governor," Bloomfield admitted, "they are protecting a group of cultists from Omaha. They are connected with one who has already been sent to Scottsbluff."

"Huh," the governor laughed. "Do you mean cultists, as in Satan and witchcraft, or do you mean fundamental Christians?"

"They are considered lawbreakers in Nebraska, Sir," Bloomfield barked.

"Yeah, I know the drill, Agent Bloomfield. Won't comply with The Church Act, guilty of hate speech, outspoken against the government, refuse to follow religious mandates, don't pay church taxes...DON'T WASTE MY TIME, BLOOMFIELD!"

Bloomfield looked confused about the governor's statements. "I have every intention of apprehending them, and taking them back to Omaha for sentencing."

The governor acted surprised. "Well, no wonder Rainwater wants to shoot you! Maybe they are not considered as criminals, under Indian laws." He paused for a moment. "So you want to use your murder investigation for other clandestine purposes, and Rainwater knows it! Is that correct?"

"Yes, damn it!" Bloomfield screamed. The governor was still composed. "If you are there to hurt his friends, fine, he should go ahead and shoot you then."

The governor then slammed a book down on the table. "Do you recognize this book, Bloomfield?"

"Yep," he answered. "King James Bible—the illegal kind!"

"It's not illegal, Bloomfield! Not yet!" The governor raised his voice. Then he smiled. "And it happens to be mine. I am a fundamental Christian, elected by the kind people of South Dakota. You are out of your league, don't you think?"

Bloomfield turned red with anger. "And the 'Church Act,' Governor?"

The governor sat back in his chair. "I don't go to the Common Church, or read the Common Bible, Bloomfield. Nor am I a registered pastor."

Bloomfield quieted down a bit. "So, you don't believe that those who defy federal law and practice religion outside of the guidelines of The Church Act—you don't believe they are cultists?"

The governor yawned. "They are friends getting together under their own roof—no different than a bridge game; and their personal views are none of your business. If they are not choosing to be registered under The Church Act, it is not your concern. You are only to concern yourself with the fools who comply with it, and don't follow the rules."

Bloomfield was visibly upset. "These renegades that Rain-what's-his-face is protecting are from the state of Nebraska! They are here illegally! They are cultists, and considered part of a government resistance group. They are under my jurisdiction, and I have the right to arrest them under Nebraska law, and I'm expecting your support, Mr. Governor!"

The governor shook his head. "I'll make it easy for you, Bloomfield. I will authorize you to conduct your murder investigation in Cedar Ridge. I will specify that all questioning be done on site, and nobody will leave the property. If any arrests are in order, you will go through due process, authorized by the Rapid City Police Department, as they see fit."

The governor opened one of his desk drawers. "They, in turn, will need authorization from me before sending any prisoners out of state. They will most likely be tried and convicted in the State of South Dakota, under South Dakota law. I'll send two uniformed officers to accompany you to Cedar Ridge. Give me 30 minutes to have it drawn up. This will be for the murder investigation, and nothing else. If you wish to pursue more than that, you will take it up with the governor of Nebraska. I venture to say, he will most likely choose not to bother with your request."

Bloomfield's face again turned red. "I don't get your logic, Governor, but you might as well draw up the papers. That'll do for now."

A half hour later, he handed Bloomfield the documents and wished him a good day, and smiled.

Bloomfield grumbled as he slammed the door on the way out.

AFTER MEETING WITH THE GOVERNOR, Bloomfield devised a plan on how he would pursue things further, so-to-speak. It would not be through the governor of Nebraska, it would be through the news media.

The news media had always been the source that could work that magic to get things stirred up on a bigger scale, regardless of which side of the fence a person was on politically, or religiously. The news media had a way to devise stories in which people were motivated to take sides. In the past, a simple story of a white policeman shooting a black youth, regardless of circumstances, could stimulate full scale racial riots within a week's time.

Although Bloomfield had to admit that he jumped out of the box when it came to the understanding of some laws. He felt a bit embarrassed and shamed by the governor. Bloomfield viewed people who read the original Bible as criminals, when technically, they were breaking no laws. If a church that was registered under the Federal Church Act taught from a "King James Bible," instead of the "Common Bible," THAT would be considered unlawful. This did not yet apply to private citizens. Also, as long as beliefs were only beliefs, no laws were broken; unless those beliefs turned into an activity, and even then it had to clearly be an unlawful activity.

Bloomfield considered a man who vowed to refuse the RFID chip a criminal. In reality, he would not be a criminal, until he actually refused it, not just because he said that he would.

What Bloomfield desired to do, had to be examined in the light of reality. Could he legally do it? Some of his professional FBI training appeared to be slipping. He'd have to tighten up a bit and become more wise and crafty. Now the question was how to come up with a good story for the news reporters—something that would make people take sides and create real problems for Cedar Ridge.

IN THE ECONOLODGE, LILLY SAT ALONE. She was more frightened than she had ever been her whole life. She had finally reached her boyfriend Charlie on her cell phone, and he said he was on his way.

He was the only one she truly trusted, besides Reverend Harris. She would tell Charlie what had happened. He always kept his cool, and the conversations that they had in private, stayed private. The sense of trust and dependability she found in Charlie was rare in a relationship. Her biggest fear now, was that he might talk her into reporting all of this to the Police. If she were to report what she knew of Agent Mattson's death, her father might somehow get out of the charge or go into hiding. If he wasn't arrested right away, he would stalk her secretly, and vow to punish her. The type of man her father was, warranted this fear. He would never forget that she had crossed him. He would attempt to ruin her, or perhaps even kill her!

Maybe Charlie would know what to do. Lilly was being tortured emotionally, while waiting for him to arrive. Finally around 9:00 p.m., he found his way to the motel.

Lilly sensed a great wave of comfort as he sat with her and held her in his arms. She cried on his shoulder, and her whole body shook, as she sobbed. "I can't believe my dad did it, Charlie, but I know he did! I don't know what to do. I'm afraid to go home, but I can't afford to be on the run when my bank credit is this low."

"What about Reverend Harris, Lil?" Charlie asked.

"I know, I know!" she cried. "I thought about that. I almost drove over to Cedar Ridge today!"

Charlie rubbed her hands. "Look, Lil, you don't want them to be blamed for what your dad did, do you?" Charlie stood before her now. "The Reverend and his friends are being protected there, Lil. I'm sure they would let you stay at Cedar Ridge where you would be safe."

"I know, Charlie," she responded. "I trust Reverend Harris, I really do! He used to come into the Café every day and talk to me about Jesus and the Bible. That's why I warned them when the FBI was snooping around. I went to Frank next door, so I guess I helped protect them. Maybe they owe me."

"It's not because they owe you, Lil," he answered, "it's because Reverend Harris cares about you."

"Do you think they'd let *you* stay, too?" Lilly asked as she dried her eyes.

Charlie took her hands again. "We'll have to see, hon. I know they would protect YOU, for sure. They need to know what happened, Lil!" He tugged at her hands. "C'mon, let's check out of here, okay? We'll go to Cedar Ridge. You have to trust SOMEONE, and Reverend Harris is the most solid guy I know."

She was reluctant to respond to his tugging, but Charlie urged her on. "Look, I want to help you, too, but the people at Cedar Ridge will keep you safe. More than I could. I also know Rainwater. I helped him one time, to get those special phones they use. He's really a nice guy, come with me, Lil. Please?"

Lilly sniffed, then blew her nose. She finally had stopped crying. "Ok, Charlie, but I want to ride with YOU. I can leave my Nissan here and someone can pick it up later, okay? Let's go now before I chicken out!"

Charlie reassured her. "You're doing the right thing, Lil. I'll get the car, while you head for the office to get checked out. Don't worry—it'll be all right."

Charlie gently took Lilly's hand. "I love you," he said softly, and Lilly finally smiled.

45

CHAPTER

THAT SAME NIGHT, TIM HARRIS STAYED UP LATE. He and the fellowship, plus some men and women from the Tee Pee Village, all met that evening at the community center. The plan was that either Tim or one of the others would share a message, and then everyone would break up into smaller groups, discuss God's Word, and pray for knowledge of His will.

Tim had a lot on his heart that particular night, and, as usual, they would pray for God's blessing, and for Tim to hear God's leading on what he should share. Many folks had been asking Tim questions about what happened to the churches, what happened to the country, and why God would bring judgments so quickly. Tim believed he was given some answers. They sat in a large circle of 25 people or so. Tim finally sat down and began to speak, after a brief prayer.

"Brothers and Sisters, I've been impressed the last few days with thoughts about God's dealings with Israel. In the Old Testament, there are several examples of a deadly cycle they fell into after their deliverance from Egypt. When God began to appoint kings to rule over them, some of those kings, such as David, had a heart for God, and had the intentions of following His will. Yet, even in Davids case, they all had sin."

"It is no different with our leaders today. Yet in our case, I doubt we will ever see a king like David ruling the country. In Israel's infancy, many kings were kings by inheritance, and many of them were evil. The evil kings often compromised when it came to the worship of other gods and idols. In most cases, those kings died, and were followed by others who had good intentions of cleaning out the idols and false worship, and bringing Israel back to its senses. But even then, many of those kings still honored the request to leave a few idols up in the hills, for people to worship. The 2 Kings 17 speaks of this. And just as Jesus later taught his disciples, 'a little leaven, leavens the whole lump,' this proved to be true every time. Not only did false gods re-emerge, but also a general rebellion against the God of Israel, the true God!

"Nehemiah 9 is a good sum up of these generations. Yet, even after the many times that Israel rebelled, God still loved them and did not allow them to perish entirely. Nehemiah 9 also concludes with that truth. In our own country, we have repeated that same cycle. Churches that once intended to follow God's Word and teach a personal relationship with a living Savior. The idols and false gods have stormed in and corrupted it. What's even worse, our leaders and government want to prevent a cleansing of this idolatry. This is what has brought God's judgement!

"When we have corruption in government, plus corruption in the so-called church, we have judgement! But, as written in Nehemiah 9, the true believers will not be cast down by God. By the world, we shall still suffer, yes. We will still be persecuted, yes. Jesus taught us all along, 'If they persecuted me, they will also persecute you.' Here at Cedar Ridge, my prayer is that we will surrender to God's love and compassion. Jesus said to His people Israel, how

He desired to gather them under His wing, the way a bird cares for her young. My prayer and hope for all of us, is to be gathered under His wings."

Tim stopped abruptly and sat back down in the circle. "Ok, let's fellowship!" And a huge smile beamed on his face.

As they began to break up into smaller groups, two men from the welcoming committee approached Tim. "Mr. Harris, Mr. Harris!" They were alarmed, to say the least. Tim turned toward them as they spoke.

"Two young people are at the gate, Reverend, a girl and a boy. They said they need to talk to you, and that it IS an emergency!"

Tim quickly followed the men outside and walked quickly to the gate. The two kids had already been admitted, and Tim recognized them right away. "Lilly? From the café?" he asked with surprise. He was a bit shocked when she ran and embraced him. It almost knocked him off his feet. She was crying hysterically! It took several minutes for Tim and Lilly's boyfriend, Charlie, to finally get her calmed down enough to talk.

Tim walked them over to Rainwater's office so they could all sit together privately. Tim tried his best to be calm and comforting. "What do you have to tell me, Lilly?"

By then, she had finally caught her breath. "The FBI guy that got killed! I know who did it!"

Tim nodded, and waited with patience as she continued to compose herself. "It was my dad, Mr. Harris! The manager at Quick Lunch told the FBI guy where I lived, because he was looking for me. I was gone the day he showed up, but my dad was home. I went home earlier today and found blood and a tire iron with blood on it. Blood was in his truck, Mr. Harris, and also on the ground!"

Tim was silent for a moment. "Did you report this to the police, Lilly?" Tim asked.

Then Charlie answered on her behalf. "Not yet, Reverend, we were both afraid it would put her life in danger, if she ratted him out. Her dad could be anywhere. Before the police catch up with him, he might kill Lilly!"

Tim reached his hands out to both of them, and smiled faintly. "Not to worry. We will put you both up for as long as we need to—you'll be safe with us, God willing."

One of the welcomers then entered the office, after overhearing some of the conversation. "Do you want me to go to town, Reverend? To call the police?"

Tim lowered his eyes to the floor. "I guess we have no other choice. I DO want to see Rainwater before you leave, though."

The Indian headed for the door. "He's still at the center—I'll go get him!"

Lilly, a bit calmer now, changed the subject. "Mr. Harris, let's talk some more about Jesus. I thought a lot about our talks in the café. Charlie and I both want to know about the real Jesus."

"Ok," Tim smiled. "We'll check with Rainwater on the police situation, real quick. Then we'll talk some more. You may have to tell your story again, but we'll talk in the meantime, and later, too, if you wish."

Lilly finally smiled. "I would love that, Mr. Harris."

Charlie sat close by her side, and took her hand. Tim prayed silently and gave God thanks.

THE RAPID CITY POLICE ENDED UP contacting Bloomfield, and, just as the governor had ordered, they sent two officers to escort him to Cedar Ridge.

The paperwork from the governor was handed over to John Rainwater, when they appeared at the gate. Just to be safe, Rainwater, Tim, Lilly, and Charlie were the only ones at the office. The rest of the believers went to Tee Pee Village, and stayed out of sight.

It seemed to Rainwater that Bloomfield was sincere, and would play by the governor's rules. Any thoughts that Bloomfield had in mind secretly, would wait till later.

After John checked the documents, he had them all admitted. Bloomfield grilled Lilly for nearly an hour, until he was convinced to take the officers to the Munson ranch to question her father; that is, if he was even there. If they were to locate him, they would arrest him first and question him later.

Bloomfield looked at Lilly and said to her, "You will need to come with me."

These words barely left his mouth, when one of the officers interrupted. "The order from the governor specifically states that all questioning takes place on site! Nobody leaves Cedar Ridge, Bloomfield!"

His face reddened a bit. "Yeah, yeah, okay. Let's step it up then, and get out to the Munson ranch and bust this animal!"

As they got up to leave the office, Bloomfield had written down the directions to the Munson residence, and held them tightly in his fist. They decided to go in Bloomfield's rented vehicle, and left the police car parked in town. They didn't want to approach the Munson residence in a marked car.

Later, when they reached the house, they found it dark, with the exception of one light still on in the kitchen. They knocked first, and when no one answered, they entered by force, breaking down the front door. Bloomfield found no one in the kitchen, but spotted Lilly's note. Next, they took a stroll around the grounds. Howard Munson's truck still remained parked in the yard, and Bloomfield was able to give it a quick going over. Everything was just as Lilly had described, including the blood stain near the door handle. The tire iron was still lying on the ground, covered with dried blood.

"So," Bloomfield barked, "It's obvious that Munson never came home since yesterday. He flew the coop so it looks like we'll have a manhunt on our hands."

In a way, this predicament delighted Bloomfield. This would be an opportunity for press coverage, and no doubt, he would be interviewed. He would say in those interviews that he was suspicious of other criminal activity, as well. Criminal activity that involved Cedar Ridge.

Bloomfield hoped to cause a firestorm. He would indicate to the press that corruption was taking place in Cedar Ridge that involved the governor himself. With any amount of luck, Bloomfield hoped to cause conflict between the Federal Government and the Indian Nation.

THE FOLLOWING MORNING, Bloomfield and the two police officers began the investigation. It was that morning that Agent Bloomfield found a goldmine of evidence that would help his campaign against Cedar Ridge. He would also have a big bone to throw to the news media.

When they went to the construction company where Howard Munson was employed, they found out that Munson did not show up for work on the day in question. Also, they found out that Munson owned no vehicles, other than his pickup truck. They came to the conclusion that he left on foot, either to hitchhike, or take a bus out of town. No cars were reported stolen, and no one knew of any friend he had that helped him.

After gleaning all they could from his place of employment, Bloomfield wanted to visit the site where Lee's body was found. It was on this excursion that Bloomfield spotted the caves. Even though the caves were on Indian land, Bloomfield assumed he had the freedom to proceed.

After a long uphill climb on the trail, he finally was able to enter the caves. He found no sign of Munson, but he was ecstatic to discover that the caves were stocked with guns and ammunition; also food, water, and other survival supplies. The caves appeared to be prepared as a fortress, built for battle. When he later returned to his hotel, he scored yet another victory.

Bloomfield called the Omaha office of the FBI, which transferred him to the Regional Office in St. Louis, who, in turn, connected him with the Central Office in Washington, D.C. The murder of an FBI agent was big business in D.C. It took no time at all to get media attention. After making and receiving a few more calls, Bloomfield found himself booked for a news conference with the major networks and cable news channels. He was scheduled for the following day, August 15.

Bloomfield was excited that one of the questions on everybody's mind would be, "What was Agent Lee Mattson investigating when he was murdered?" Bloomfield could hardly wait to answer that one! Was it, Cedar Ridge protecting wanted criminals for crimes and conspiracies against the Federal Government? Or, the governor of South Dakota's refusal to allow Bloomfield to follow up on those leads. Or was it the discovery of caves stocked with weapons, in which Bloomfield was careful to leave the evidence exactly as he found it! The fact that the Indian Nation of Cedar Ridge thought they had authority over the FBI, and had threatened to kill him if he returned. Also, the fact that the governor heartily agreed with Rainwater!

"Bring it on!" Bloomfield laughed, and spoke out loud. He also knew that even if the entire town of Rapid City were fundamental Christians like their governor, they would be far outnumbered by National public opinion. Most of the nation fell on their knees before The Church Act. Mostly out of fear, and many out of respect for the law, whether right or wrong. "This means war!" Bloomfield bellowed. "Cedar Ridge will be finished!"

ON THE AFTERNOON OF AUGUST 15TH, over 20 million people in America were watching WNNN, the National News Network. At 5:00 p.m. Eastern time, Bloomfield's interview was to be aired. He was stoked, and quite elated that he was interviewed by Cindy Patterson during the taping of the show. Cindy was in Bloomfield's corner. She was a big supporter of the Common Bible and The Church Act.

A thin blonde woman sat at the anchor desk as large letters streamed across the screen which read, "Breaking Story." The anchor smiled as the camera zoomed in—then she turned solemn.

"In a breaking news today, we are focusing on a growing crisis in the small community of Cedar Ridge, South Dakota, where an Omaha, Nebraska FBI Agent, Lee Mattson, was murdered five days ago. Cedar Ridge, which is a Native American reservation, was the general area where Agent Mattson's body was found. This tragedy has now been escalating into a crisis that goes as deep as the Governor's office."

"We now take you live to Cindy Patterson on the scene near Cedar Ridge. Cindy?"

Cindy appeared on the screen. "Yes, Barbara, I'm standing near the location where the agent's body was found. Agent Lee Mattson was brutally beaten to death. With me is Agent Lawrence Bloomfield of the Omaha FBI office. Agent Bloomfield, can you tell us some background about Agent Mattson's visit and purpose in South Dakota?"

Lawrence's face then filled the screen. "Yes, Cindy, Agent Mattson and myself had been investigating the whereabouts of some fugitives from Nebraska. These individuals were cultists involved in an underground resistance group. Mattson and I concluded that they were hiding out on Indian land in the community of Cedar Ridge, based on reliable evidence we obtained."

Cindy's face reappeared. "And does this have a direct bearing on Agent Mattson's murder?"

Bloomfield again. "Yes, it does, Cindy. Agent Mattson arrived in the town center to question a waitress named Lilly Munson, who worked for the Quick Lunch café. Agent Mattson considered her a suspect who had aided in the escape of the cultists, when we came here to investigate two weeks earlier. When Agent Mattson arrived at the home where she lived, he was confronted and murdered by her father, Howard Munson." Howard Munson's picture was then shown on the screen. "Munson is still at large," Bloomfield continued. "We are now offering a reward of $10,000 in bank credit for any valid tip that would lead to his arrest!"

Cindy's face returned. "You mentioned to me before we went on the air that you also made another discovery at this location?"

Bloomfield smiled. "Yes, Cindy, that's right. Just about 100 yards behind us is a cluster of caves, located high up in the cliffs." The camera pointed in that direction, revealing three small cave openings in the distance. "These caves were stocked with weapons and ammunition, along with survival provisions. Those caves are located on Indian land, and overseen by the residents of Cedar Ridge."

"Mr. Bloomfield," The camera panned back to Cindy, "Can you tell us why it is now so difficult to apprehend the cultists?"

Bloomfield chuckled. "First I was told by the director in charge of Cedar Ridge, Mr. John Rainwater, that Native American Law on Native land, was protected from government interference, and if I tried to force my authority to apprehend their friends, they would shoot me!"

Cindy nodded. "I then took the matter to the governor of the state. He gave me legal authorization to investigate the murder of my agent, but nothing more. I was not even given permission to make arrests, but only to question suspects. When I told the governor the situation regarding the cultists, he laughed about it! He said they had broken no laws in South Dakota. The governor told me point blank that if I tried to use force in order to make those arrests, he would have no problem with them shooting me, even though the cultists were neither Native Americans, nor South Dakota residents. He believed I had no right to make the arrests and return them to Nebraska for trial."

Cindy now appeared on the screen. "So these fugitives are still in Cedar Ridge, Sir?" She then added, "Well, let me also ask this, as well—what exactly are they guilty of?"

Bloomfield looked toward the ground. "They are still in Cedar Ridge, yes! I cannot go as far as to explain the details of their crimes, but I assure you it will be brought to light when they are arrested and sentenced."

Cindy then ended the interview and thanked Bloomfield. The news station went on to other top stories. Bloomfield was delighted with the broadcast. He was expecting the Cedar Ridge crisis to quickly escalate, because of the news exposure.

Bloomfield was also informed by the FBI Headquarters that 50 agents would be sent to Cedar Ridge to assist him. The 50 agents had the authorization by federal law to enter Cedar Ridge, by force, if necessary.

ON THE 15TH, RONNIE GREENLEAF of the welcoming committee knocked and entered John Rainwater's office. He reported to Rainwater that the news media was all over the area. More than one network, and still growing. "I could see everything through my rifle scope," he said. "I could zoom right in on Bloomfield's face. Could've capped him right there, if I wanted to."

Rainwater turned angry. "Don't ever talk like that in this office, Ron! We do nothing except in self-defense! Don't forget it!" Rainwater then sat back with his hands behind his head. "Did anyone hear the broadcast?"

"Yeah," Ronnie grunted. "Reverend Harris saw it. He told me they did a great job making us all look like terrorists!"

"They made it look like Bloomfield was on a mission to save the country!" Ronnie started pacing the floor, angrily. "Bloomfield blasted the governor, too. Tim said he wouldn't be surprised if the governor was to be arrested along with everybody else!"

Rainwater signed when he heard this. "I wonder what the next move will be?"

Ronnie slammed a clip of ammo into his rifle. "Since more news guys keep showing up, that's a good sign that they are expecting something to hit the fan soon! I'll keep guards on the gate, John."

Rainwater sighed again, then stood. "Ronnie, you look like you're enjoying this too much. Keep in mind that Tim and his friends are being targeted for no other reason than teaching the love of God through Jesus. We are not killers and this is not a time for us to make vengeance. You are all standing guard, only as a protective measure. This is tragic, and it's happening all over America, not just here."

"Uh, huh!" Ronnie sneered. "I'll keep the guards on duty, John!" Ronnie Greenleaf then left the office with his weapon loaded and ready. He slammed the door violently behind him as he left.

Jennifer had just finished a session of school and gracefully entered her husband's office. She put her gentle arms around him to comfort him. "I know this is probably not a good time to tell you that everything will work out. The fact is, it might not. Not in the physical world, anyway. All things belong to God, Johnny, we've been bought with a price." She held her husband tighter. "All we can do is surrender to the Lord, by faith. And hey—I love you, Johnny!"

"And I love you, too, Jen!" he answered. "Hey, has Billy Whitebird been doing any drawings?"

"That's strange, John," she answered. "He still keeps drawing that cross, and saying the word "trust" over and over. He didn't show up at school today. His mother told me when she dropped by this morning that he wouldn't be at school, because he went to visit the Spirit cave."

Rainwater patted her hand. "He'll be okay, Jen. He's probably the only one in this whole village that has a handle on things. He looked up, "So, what's on the agenda for tonight?"

"A meeting here at the school room." She answered. "Just you, me, Stu, Phil, Todd, and the Freemans will be providing the dinner. Susan and Angela, will be there, too, of course; and Tim, by popular demand."

"What about the new guests, Lilly and Charlie?"

"Now, that is a surprise, and you'll just have to wait, Mr. Rainwater!" She smiled.

Johnny finally stood up and stretched. "Guess I better hit the shower and try to get an hour's nap." Jennifer also yawned and stretched. "You need help with that nap?" They both laughed.

THAT NIGHT ABOUT 7:00 P.M., people began knocking on the office door. Everyone arrived, including Frank, Gabe, Lilly, and Charles. They all gathered together in the school room. Joe and Margaret Freeman brought a wonderful chicken noodle casserole made from home-made egg noodles, slowly cooked in a crock pot. Rainwater was looking forward to the surprise that Jennifer had told him to expect.

Once everyone enjoyed a fine meal, Tim asked for everybody's attention. "This is a special occasion, folks!" he said. "I'm going to turn things over to Lilly, at this time."

Lilly and Charlie were seated close together and beaming with joy. "Well, I'm not so hot at speakin'," Lilly began, "so I hope you don't mind if I don't give any elaborate speeches, but the thing is this, Charlie and I both accepted the Lord Jesus as our Savior today!" Everyone in the room shouted with joy, and applauded. "I guess Jesus really found us, because we were just talking together like normal, and the subject of God came up. We decided to open the Bible to a random page, just to see what it would say. When we read it, it was not just a Bible any more. We heard God's voice in our hearts, and suddenly our eyes were opened, and we believed, just like that! Also, we were not afraid anymore."

"What scripture did you read, Honey?" Margaret asked.

"It was in 1 John. It said, 'And the witness is this, that God has given us eternal life, and this life is in His son. He who has the Son has the life; he who does not have the Son of God does not have the life. These things I have written to you who believe in the Name of the Son of God, in order that you may know that you have eternal life.' When we read this, we both remembered the things Reverend Harris told us about the cross and resurrection. Suddenly we knew it was all true." She sat down in silence.

Then Charlie said, "We both know about the danger we are all in right now, but when Jesus saved us, it seems like it doesn't really matter anymore. We understand now that real life is not in this world. Real life is in heaven with Jesus." He cleared his throat. "Mary also read us some things from the book of Romans, which made things even more clear than ever."

"How's Mary doing, anyway?" Phil asked.

Charlie then answered, "Oh, she's doing fine. She hasn't been around that much, because she's spending time with Angela in Tee Pee Village. Tonight she had promised to babysit some kids, so that's why she isn't here right now. She'll probably spend the night there, I suppose."

Then all the believers gathered around for some cherry pie. They enjoyed dessert and fellowship together. Hardly anyone mentioned the FBI threat. God gave them a peace that passed understanding—a peace that does not come from this world.

ON THE MORNING OF THE 18TH, things were tense at the entry gate to the reservation, because Federal Law could override State Law, and the governor of South Dakota was overruled in his efforts to protect Cedar Ridge.

The 50 agents from the FBI were authorized to report to the location from Washington, D.C. The order was signed by the President himself.

The news media crowded near the entrance area. News reporters numbered in the hundreds.

Rainwater sat alone in his office, baffled. He was baffled not so much because of the executive order for the FBI to enter the village, as he was about Tim Harris not inviting him to an emergency meeting of the believers. Jennifer had not been invited either, because she was his wife.

The meeting was taking place in the schoolroom. The office entry door was closed for privacy. Everyone attended, except Rainwater and Jennifer. Tim, Stu, Phil, Todd, the Freemans, Gabe, Frank, Mary, Angela, Susan, plus the new believers, Lilly and Charlie. Thirteen all together.

The meeting seemed to go on forever. Both Rainwater and Jennifer were growing impatient.

By noon, the FBI agents that were sent to assist Bloomfield were beginning to arrive and assemble themselves right outside the main gate. They all carried weapons.

Finally Tim and the others emerged from the schoolroom and crowded into Rainwater's office. None of them spoke. Tim sat down at Rainwater's desk, and motioned him over. Tim spoke softly and humbly to Johnny.

"We realize, John, that the whole village is in danger of slaughter. We also heard that units from the National Guard will be arriving soon. It was announced on the news this morning. We discussed this among ourselves, and have come to a decision."

Rainwater leaned forward toward Tim. Johnny had a look of horror on his face. He knew what Tim was about to propose.

"John, we have decided to surrender. It would possibly save the village. We are the only ones here that aren't Native Americans, with the exception of Jennifer, because she is your wife. The Lord gave us a message from His Word that greater love has no man than this—that he lay down his life for his friends. We also found the passage in Philippians 2, which basically says we are to empty ourselves the same way Jesus did on our behalf. He went willingly to the cross, because of God's great love for us. God has given us peace to do the same for this village, and our friends. We will walk out to the gate, and discuss the deal with Bloomfield. Don't try to hold us back, Johnny—the decision is made."

Rainwater leaned over the desk and took ahold of Tim's arms and began to weep. Jennifer joined in. Strangely enough, John Rainwater did not speak, but just nodded to indicate that he understood God's will, and would honor Tim's request.

Rainwater turned and looked at the other 12 believers, then spoke: "I love you. If God has spoken this to your hearts, then I know you must go. Jen and I will continue to teach God's Word to this village. I will still pray that same prayer Jesus prayed before he went to the cross—that this cup may pass from you. Yet I also will remember His words, 'Yet, not my will be done, but Thine.'"

Then the 13, including Tim, left the office and walked toward the gate. They all knew they were possibly walking toward their deaths. But God had promised them eternal life and settled their hearts with His everlasting love and peace that only believers in Christ could know.

"God forgive them, for they know not what they do." Phil quoted the words of Christ, as they walked on. Jesus had said these words from the cross. He was mocked, He was slandered and beaten, then He was crucified; and even then, the gift of forgiveness flowed from His mouth.

In the end, Bloomfield accepted the offer. He also allowed Jennifer to remain as Rainwater's wife. The Cedar Ridge believers were not sent to Scottsbluff, Nebraska. They were escorted to the location where Lee's body had been found, and executed there. They went home peacefully, and quickly. The nation was shocked. It brought fear to many who saw it on the news that night. For the believers at Cedar Ridge...*they'd found their real home at last.*

EPILOGUE

THIRTEEN DAYS LATER, ON THE 31ST OF AUGUST, Patty Miller knelt before her metal sleeping bunk to say her prayers. The small cold prison cell disappeared from her thoughts, as the love and grace of God fell upon her. She could sense God's embrace. At 11:45 a.m., a guard entered her cell and spoke the words she knew she would hear.

"Patty Miller! It's time! You must come with me now!" His voice had the sound of a grim reaper, yet she stood firmly as the cuffs were placed on her wrists.

"I'm ready." She answered.

THE END